The Ninth Race

The Ninth Race

A Mike Flint Murder Mystery

By R. Austin Healy

The Marshall Jones Co.
Publishers Since 1902
Manchester Center, Vermont

Library of Congress Catalog
Card Number 94-076337

I.S.B.N. 0-8338-0211-9

Printed in the United States of America

Dedication:

To Siro's, a special place where
Saratoga's finest gather each August.

An Acknowledgement:

No book is developed entirely by its author.
So I extend my gratitude to Matt Graves, who
originally edited my rough draft; the late Eleanor
Lambert who first introduced me to word pro-
cessing; Joe LaMora, a wizard on his computer
who helped me piece it all together; to Dennis
Johnson and Jeni Stewart for their jacket de-
sign; to Shirley Jones and my wife, Joan, for their
proofreading and to publishers Peggi Simmons
and Craig Altschul of the Marshall Jones Co. who
had faith in the book's viability.

This is a work of fiction. While the places are
generally real, any resemblance to people or
events is purely coincidental and come directly
from my own imagination.

• *R. Austin Healy, 1994,*
Saratoga Springs, New York

CONTENTS

The Ninth Race

1. Robin's Nest

She walked down the dimly lit hallway to the small bathroom, turned on the wall light and stared at the odd-shaped Victorian tub. Robin preferred a shower stall, but there was none. The porcelain tub was too short for her five-foot eight body, and it was difficult to shampoo and rinse her long blond hair. She turned on the hot water and proceeded to clean the sides before filling it for her bath.

It sputtered at first, then settled to a steady downpour, the vapor rising from the tub, helping to warm the room so that she could disrobe and stand facing the wall mirror in relative comfort.

She lifted a brush to intractable hair, tugging at stringy locks that seemed to fight back each stroke until, finally, her wrist grew tired and she realized that brushing was useless until after her shampoo.

Underneath her feet the floor squeaked. In fact, everything squeaked in the old mansion, a once proud home turned rooming house to fit the economics of the times. It was all she could afford, at least temporarily. She knew she would probably have to tolerate these conditions for some time and, thinking about it, a quiet melancholy came over her; a legacy from her past.

Robin never remembered it being any differ-ent. As a child she had suffered through years of near poverty. Her father never held a steady job and her mother worked when she could, but bad health kept her bedridden most of the time. When she was eleven her mother died and her father, unable to care for her, decided she should live with her Aunt Helen and Uncle Mark on their small farm in Waycross, Georgia.

Helen and Mark showed true affection which helped during the difficult time. She made the adjustment to the farm quite easily, though the pain of her mother's death stayed with her for months. Leaving her father hadn't the slightest effect on Robin, she could show no emotion where he was concerned.

The normalcy of three meals a day, getting the proper sleep and attending school regularly took some getting used to, but eventually every-thing had fallen into place. For the first time in her young life she felt like a whole person. Be-cause of her shyness, her social life was a bit limited, and it continued that way through most of her school years, although she had finally at-tended a few functions at Aunt Helen's insistence, including her senior prom.

She slipped into the tub, slowly letting the warm water come to her mid-section before curl-ing back so that it reached her neckline and cov-ered her shoulders. She poured bath powder and watched as it foamed about her body. Her hands ran along her legs, massaging the skin, pushing the day's dirt free and relaxing her tired muscles.

Outside, the stiff February wind lashed against the narrow bathroom window. The or-nate iron radiator in the corner began to rattle and shake, its metallic innards hissing eerie noises; sounds that often woke her during the night as heat was suddenly pumped through the antiquated system, a system designed and installed when Saratoga was a young, more opulent city.

Robin had departed the warmth and reassurance of Mark and Helen when she was nineteen, to marry a soldier from Fort Benning who she scarcely knew. Yet, it all seemed very right and beautiful at the time. After having held back her emotions for so long, she suddenly found herself deliriously in love.

The startling discovery that she had made a bad choice did not come until they had been married nearly two years and she had given birth to a baby daughter, Sara. Her husband Ron, 27, was into alcohol and drugs. He didn't respond to help, so the army gave him a medical discharge. Their marriage ended in divorce. She could have gone back to Mark and Helen, but she was too embarrassed, too ashamed of herself and her failed marriage.

Taking Sara, she headed north to New York City. Her first interview was for a secretarial job at Bellevue Hospital. The job didn't materialize; nevertheless she stayed on in New York, searching the job market for a solid month, willing to take any kind of employment, any small meaningless job that would pay the rent and put food on the table for her and Sara.

Look, honey," one man told her. "This is no place for a young girl with a kid. Go back where you came from. New York is too big, too hard, too lousy a hole for someone like you. Do yourself a favor, go back to wherever it is you came from." She didn't take his advice and continued to look for work. Within two months time, she found herself penniless, standing in line at a Catholic Charity house. A small round hand held out a pen and a piece of paper for her to fill out. She sat at a bench and filled in the necessary information, printing her name slowly -- Robin Johnson -- then, realizing she wasn't married anymore, changed it back to her maiden name.

"We don't normally take in children here," said the tall nun in charge. "We have other places that take on that responsibility."

"I can't leave my daughter!" said Robin, tears welling in her eyes. Then smiling, the nun said, "We'll make an exception this time, but you must understand, we have limited space and many waiting for help so it can only be for a few days at most."

Robin remembered looking back in bewildered hopelessness, saying, "I'll find work soon, I promise."

The water was cooling down a bit. She opened the drain and let some out, then turning the faucet, let fresh hot water flow into the tub. Laying back, soaking up the newly flowing warmth, she began to apply shampoo to her hair, rubbing her fingers hard against the scalp, especially at the base of her neck where the muscles were tightest. She thought of the half-finished doll in her room down the hall. She thought about Sara and wondered what she was doing at this very moment, in Georgia with Mark and Helen. So sweet of them to take her, as they had taken Robin, herself, years earlier. They would protect her, give her a good home, the proper environment. She would pay them back some day for their kindness and love. It would take time, but she would find a way to pay them back. She would find her niche and in time she would be with her daughter. They would have their own home, which she would turn into a showplace.

She had taken great patience with the doll, sewing the face so that large dimples showed -- much like Sara's. Using the sharp pencil to trace the eyes, stitching all seams twice so it wouldn't come apart. At night she would hold the doll, pretending it was Sara, talking with it, telling her about the day's activities; sometimes saying nightly prayers with it, like she had with Sara. Then she remembered that Sara's birthday was coming in April. Robin decided she would have to finish making the dress and shoes and fix the hair. The doll had to be in the mail and arrive on time for Sara's big day. She decided she would do it first thing in the morning and would let nothing interrupt her. Yes, she would get to it in the morning, right after she made her daily phone call to the special coded number in New York City to report to Harry. Tomorrow would be a day set aside for Sara's doll.

Thick, foamy lather encircled her head as her fingers pressed and tossed the hair from side to side. The water, still warm, seemed to caress her entire being, warming her throughout, and she soaked herself in a dreamlike state, wishing that it would never end.

She thought of how diluted her life had been these past few months. How, had she not gone to New York City, things might have been different. Surely there was work in Waycross. Why hadn't she swallowed her pride when the marriage had ended?

New York City was the pits. She found little to like about it during her brief stay at the shelter. In fact, the shelter with its warm atmosphere and caring nuns who looked over her and Sara with a devotion she didn't truly comprehend, was the only place that didn't madden her. Every other facet of the city sickened her, from the pimps on the corner who made rude gestures when she went out looking for work, to the pitiful filth and litter of the streets.

Finally in desperation she had taken a job waitressing at a sleazy Third Avenue bar, report-

edly a hangout for prostitutes and dope push-
ers. She didn't dare tell the nuns the truth about
her employment. She had them thinking she was
going to work at a high-rise cafeteria located in
midtown Manhattan.

She worked the day shift at first. Eventually
it led to evenings. There was a marked difference
in the bar's clientele between the day and night
time hours. Young girls painted to the hilt hung
around during the day, often dashing quickly to
a waiting car or cab, only to return a short time
later to wait for another trick. At night the girls
were replaced with older, rather well-dressed ladies. Businessmen in suits and ties came in after dark as well, had a drink or two and left with
a lady of their choice.

The bar, known as *"The Willows,"* was nothing more than a staging area. Robin went about
her work almost innocently ignorant of her surroundings.

Smoke had always bothered her. She never
touched a cigarette. *The Willows* was always filled
with smoke. When she would return from work
to the shelter, the first thing she did was to take
a long, hot shower. She would stand there for
several minutes letting the stiff spray wash away
the clammy stifling layers of filth that permeated
her hair, the pores of her skin; cigar smoke, marijuana stench, cheap perfumes, stale beer and a
hundred other distasteful smells. In time the
nuns, smelling her when she came in, knew, but
said nothing. She was allowed to stay and she
was saving money. Sara was well looked after,
and had become very fond of the nuns.

Robin reached once again for the faucet and
added still more hot water to the tub, at the same
moment a car door clicked shut out on Saratoga's
Broadway, a sound she neither heard nor would
have paid attention to if she had.

A male figure, dressed in a gray overcoat, dark hat and shiny black pointed boots with rubber soles, gazed up at the light in the narrow bathroom window. A nasty little man who was on a mission. His eyes swept first right then left up and down the cold, snowless street and, seeing no one, he moved to the rear of the mansion and headed for the fire escape. He walked like a marionette, in quick measured steps.

Wallowing in the pleasure and warmth of the tub, Robin's thoughts turned to her colleagues in New York City; to the men who had talked her into becoming a "Snitch Bitch" as the whores used to refer to street informers. She had been roped into this position, though they made it appear otherwise, insisting almost from the start that she was a willing volunteer. She remembered the circumstances very well. The night at work when her boss, Johnnie, asked her to do him a favor and deliver two bottles of scotch just around the corner. She had never been asked to deliver anything before.

"Just drop these off, Babe," said Johnnie. "And don't forget to collect forty bucks and hurry back."

She made the delivery, having to walk up two flights to the apartment. A tall, slim, flashy-dressed pimp whom she recognized from *The Willows* met her at the door. He smiled and invited her inside, an offer she declined. While she waited to get paid she could hear the voices of several men and women from within the apartment; they all sounded very drunk. Robin knew they were into drugs at this party. She smelled the strong, sweet scent of marijuana through the partly opened door. Marijuana was common among this crowd, and the pimps distributed it freely among their girls. But inside, out of sight, probably in one of the rear bedrooms, cocaine and other hard drugs were no doubt being used, also. It made her very uneasy.

After what seemed to be a long time, the pimp returned, his teeth protruding through a cheer-less, drug-effected smile, and handed her two twenty dollar bills. He then gave her another twenty as he ran his eyes over the length of her body. "Keep the extra one, doll. Spend it wisely. You know?"

Robin remembered turning to the stairs with-out even thanking him and starting down, mov-ing as quickly as she could go. As she reached the lower hallway the front door suddenly opened and three large men appeared. One had a flash-light.

The light was directed at her face and be-hind the blinding glare a rough voice asked, "Where's the party, Miss?"

She could only manage a muffled, frightened reply, "I - I - I don't know. I was on an errand."

"Fine," said the same rough voice. "Show us where."

"I have to get back to work," Robin said. "I work at *The Willows*, ask anyone."

"We're not interested, Miss."

There was a mass of confusion as more men entered the hallway, the ones in front dressed in street clothes, those following were uniformed cops. They moved up the steps, bounded through the apartment door and arrested everyone inside. It was over in minutes.

Robin had encountered her first drug bust, and subsequently found herself at Police Head-quarters along with the flashily-dressed pimp and his entourage from the apartment. She later learned that it was a sort of recruiting party, meant to introduce new girls to the easy life, with a little loosening up from drugs first.

Outside on the fire escape the solitary figure

pulled himself upward until he reached the second floor landing. There were no storm windows on the mansion, and the large-paned frames had no locks. He had no difficulty entering the old building. He slipped quickly and silently into the hallway, a draft of cold air following him in as he quietly closed the window.

Suddenly the bathroom seemed cooler, Robin thought, perhaps the heat was acting up again? Then the radiator rattled once more and she smiled; there it goes, the *Old Betsy*.

Then she thought of Sandy, her nurse friend. Robin and Sandy were to have had lunch today. But Robin didn't make it; a trying day. She had the feeling right along that someone out there on the streets of Saratoga knew what she was up to. There was the fear that Harry would pull her in, but the thought of losing her income was even more frightening. No, she would not tell him. Instead, she wrote a note to Sandy. Robin and Sandy occasionally left notes for one another, usually when it was inconvenient to get together to talk in person.

Robin generally left her notes with the hospital receptionist; however, this time she decided to leave a note with Benson, the hospital maintenance man. Simple, honest Benson was always dependable. Robin also had a notebook. She took a further precaution and put it in a Greyhound Terminal locker behind the *Spa City Diner*. She mentioned this to Sandy in her note. Hell, she thought, I'm probably overreacting. It's probably all for nothing.

The shiny pointed boots moved slowly along the hallway, some ten feet now from the bathroom. The nasty little man could hear her splashing, her breathing. As he moved forward he slipped on a pair of leather gloves. He moved without making a sound, inching along as he ap-

proached the door so that the floor didn't squeak.

Following her arrest in New York her entire life seemed to fall apart for a time. Johnnie at *The Willows* wouldn't answer her phone calls. She finally realized that Johnnie would stay a comfortable distance from this situation, no matter what his personal feelings; he walked a thin line with the cops as it was. Robin had to make two appearances in court, and no doubt would have been charged, had it not been for the nuns coming to her aid. The Mother Superior of the shelter knew a young Irish Public Defender, Mike O'Connor, and he managed to have the drug charges dropped.

Then the final blow came. The nuns at the shelter had no choice but to ask her to leave -- very reluctantly, but unequivocally. Sara cried as they departed, with virtually everything they owned, onto the big city streets.

So she found herself free, but homeless, down to two hundred dollars in savings --jobless-- with little hope of finding another job in a hurry. She and Sara stayed in the cheapest hotel she could find, taking extra caution to brace a chair against the door at night, even though it was locked. She began to make the rounds again on the job circuit, but to no avail. It was then she met the man called Harry and his associate known as Lester. They didn't give out last names. As she sat having a cup of coffee in a small restaurant, the two men just moved in and sat beside her, startling her with their uninvited presence.

She looked up nervously at the big round face with a cigar hanging out of its mouth. "I'm Harry," said the man, blowing a stream of smoke past her face.

She flared at him. "I don't understand. Who are you?" "This is my friend, Lester," said Harry. "We work together. We're a team, you might say."

Robin eyed them suspiciously. "Let's get down to some straight talk," said Harry, removing the cigar. "You got yourself in a bit of a jam this week. Isn't that so?"

Robin paused, waiting for him to go on. He stared at her.

Finally she said, "I don't know who you really are, Harry, and I certainly don't go around providing explanations to strangers."

"I can be a friend," he said quickly. "I have information that tells me you could use a good friend right now."

She pondered this statement for a moment, watching him as he moved the cigar from one side of his mouth to the other, without taking his eyes off her.

"It was all a big mistake," said Robin eventually.

"And it cost you your job," he insisted. "Didn't it?"

"It wasn't much of a job."

"It paid the rent."

"I've got better qualifications," Robin observed, "I'll land something much better."

Harry smiled a rare smile. "Well, maybe we can help you."

"How is that?"

"To begin with we can get you some employment."

Robin looked into his face calmly. "You don't appear to be businessmen. What kind of employment are you talking about?"

"We'll get into that later," said Harry.

"OK," said Robin, "I'll play it your way."

The mustached Lester leaned forward and stared at her. "Perhaps you don't understand your position."

"What do you mean," said Robin.

"You're free on the drug bust," insisted Lester.

"But you're not free to go anyplace outside of New York City. Is that clear?"

"No," Robin piped up, "that's not clear at all."

"Well, honey, it goes something like this. There's still an investigation going on about the others, and you may be needed to testify."

She drew a deep breath. "Mike O'Connor said I was free. The charges were dropped. That's all I know."

"Ya, that's right. Unmistakably right," said Harry. "Free to leave the court and to stay out of jail, but not the city. If you don't believe me, call Mike O'Connor and ask him yourself."

"I might just do that," said Robin defiantly.

"I've got his number right here," Lester interjected. "His private number. Give him a call."

Robin suddenly knew it was all tied in, that Harry, Lester and Mike O'Connor, and probably sweet little Johnnie, had set her up from the beginning. She didn't know why nor understand it, but the connection was there, and she was a product of these unscrupulous schemers, whoever they really were. Cops maybe, she could sense that.

"I understand you have a young daughter," said Lester, in a voice that implied he already knew the answer.

"You know I have a daughter," she said shakily.

"Well," continued Lester, "the job we have in mind will take some real resourcefulness, and you won't be able to do it with a kid to look after. Perhaps you got relatives -- family of some type that could look after the kid for a time?"

"I've got an uncle and aunt in Georgia, but that would be asking a little much of them. They're getting on in years."

They insisted it would be in her best interest to work it out.

14

"After all," Harry told her, "you're in a difficult position. We're the only real hope you
have--don't you agree?"

She looked at him, but didn't reply.

As always, Mark and Helen agreed to assist
her. They took Sara without reservation, and
without questioning Robin's motives. Harry gave
Robin an advance to pay for transportation, meals
and some new clothing for Sara and herself.

Robin's employment began the day she returned to New York. Harry pulled no punches
about her job. She would be a paid informer,
dealing mostly with the drug traffickers. He considered her perfect for the job, not for her intelligence, which Harry deemed mediocre, but rather
for her ability to mix with the city's community
while not being obvious.

Harry had her working in an assortment of
places throughout the city, and he moved her no
less than every five or six days so she would not
be detected.

Harry's decision to move Robin north to
Saratoga came as a surprise for she had only
been on the street two months when Harry told
her about it. He sweetened the offer with more
money. Little was said about exactly how long
her stay in Saratoga would be, nor just what her
involvement would entail. She was finding out
quickly that in most dealings with Harry and
Lester, it was mostly what they didn't say that
was the important thing.

She turned the faucet once more, deciding to
soak a bit longer. As she leaned forward a cold
draft swept across her back and head, then the
sudden realization that someone was entering
the bathroom...

*A hand gripped her head, its fingers fastening
tightly in her hair; she struggled to sit back up
but couldn't. She saw the shiny, pointed shoes*

15

out of the corner of one eye, but nothing else. The hand pressed down harder and she felt her face being driven beneath the white foamy water. Her arms reached back and grabbed for the hand holding her under, but she couldn't release it. She held her breath while trying to twist her body to one side, but the grip was like a vise.

He held her under for two or three minutes until the air in her lungs finally gushed from her mouth, and when she tried to breathe there was a long, hollow sucking sound as the lathered water invaded her body.

Down she sank, her mind still functioning though life itself was quickly ebbing from her naked soapy body held firmly in a watery death pool.

She saw Sara's face for a moment. Her daughter was reaching out both hands, beckoning her to lift herself out of the water. Then she saw Mark and Helen reaching for her, but they couldn't quite make it -- and Harry, calling from afar, telling her to get out of the tub. Her body stilled and a slow series of air bubbles rose to the top, and then everything in the bathroom was silent.

Her assassin released his grip. Robin's lifeless body sank further down so that her head was completely submerged, except for some strands of blond hair that drifted upward and lay on the water like wild sea grass.

The nasty little man watched a moment longer, making certain she was dead. Then he quickly retreated down the hallway and, in catlike silence, went out the same window he had entered, leaving behind her grotesque corpse.

A short time later, a female tenant found the body and went screaming into the cold and windy Saratoga night. When the police responded to the scene, all the water had seeped from the tub and Robin was wrapped in a web-like soapy veil.

2. Little Old Saratoga

I t was his movie-star, sometimes sleep-in-lover Monica speaking. Her blue eyes twinkled down at him as he lay back on the bed, his hands tucked beneath his head.

"I must be going Flint; after all, I have to be at the studio before seven."

She had known Flint for a dozen years, and had always considered him special. At times she even felt she was in love with him. Yet occasional long evenings, making love to a few other selected men, was acceptable to her. In the acting business, both as a young hopeful and then as a seasoned performer, she viewed certain indiscretions as a career necessity.

Her special affection for Flint bothered her, for she knew too well his line of work was dangerous and unpredictable. She could never bring herself to accept the fact that a guy as nice as Flint could continue in such a risky occupation. When alone with him she became very sentimental; her best defense at these moments was to leave.

His eyes locked with hers and he motioned her back to the bed. She shook her head and went to the chair to get her dress. It was a soft, pink satin dress, and he watched her pull it on slowly and carefully adjust it so that no wrinkles showed. Her long blonde hair trailed down her back. She had everything to charm a man with, he was thinking, and he wondered how she acted and made love to the others. It wasn't a jealous thought; he was just inquisitive.

"When will I see you again, Monica?"

"I'm very busy the rest of this week," she replied. "I'll try to call you on Saturday." She leaned over the bed and gave him a long, soft kiss. Her hair was a bit disheveled but she looked radiantly beautiful, he thought. She was pushing forty, but she could pass for twenty-five.

She smiled down at him. "As always, it was sweet. Good-bye, Flint," she said, and left.

He listened as she started the car and drove off. He went from the bed to the window as the car wound its way down the steep, narrow road and headed for Los Angeles. He could hear the Pacific Ocean surf licking the shoreline at Palos Verdes Cove just below the bluff where his cottage was situated. The sea before him was black, yet the night was clear. He looked again down the road till she was gone, the lights of L.A. visible in the distance.

He returned to bed and fell asleep.

In a dream he heard ringing. Faint at first, then louder and louder. He was in a strange far-away monastery running down a long corridor, being chased by a band of monks who were all waving little cowbells, and all shouting at him to get dressed. The ringing became louder and louder, almost deafening. The monks kept chasing after him until he finally fell down from exhaustion. Then they stood over him ringing their bells. He sat up in bed, opened his eyes and shook his head from side to side--then he realized the telephone was ringing.

Flint recognized the voice at once. It was Harry Waite calling from New York, and he knew immediately that it would probably be an assignment, and undoubtedly an unpleasant one at that. Seldom did Harry call him on anything but ugly affairs...

Harry's voice took on that sneakingly solicitous tone when the job was particularly difficult. Mike had been through this verbal manipulating many times before. Still, he didn't refuse or question Harry up front. Experience had taught him that it was always wiser to let Harry talk himself out first.

Flint knew Harry all too well. Harry was not your conventional cop -- never had been. He did everything his way. You always dealt with him knowing this fact. At fifty years of age and carrying 240 pounds -- mostly around his beltline -- Harry couldn't move fast enough for street duty, so they had stuck him behind a desk years ago. Nevertheless, he possessed a quick mind and a toughness few men have, and you knew he was no one to fool with when he looked at you with his small, narrowly set, iron-gray eyes. It was those piercing eyes Mike Flint always remembered. You just couldn't think of Harry without recalling his eyes. There was something sinister about them.

"You're the man for this one, Mike," Harry was saying over the phone. "I thought of you first. I'd like to think you'll accept this job." Flint could tell Harry was speaking with a cigar in his mouth. "You're well respected at Central," Harry said, trying to sound genuine.

"Skip the B.S., Harry."

"No. I mean it, Mike. They have nothing but praise for you."

"Fine, Harry. I'll treasure their thoughts."

"I gave this call a lot of consideration before making it," said Harry. "I wasn't going to call you at first, but then I couldn't think of anyone better suited to help me out."

Flint could picture the big face at the other end of the line, with that deep, unyielding voice. And he suddenly remembered smoldering assignments from the past that he had so diligently pursued for Harry and Central. So many different kinds of ventures. Murder, drugs, diamond heist, mob rubouts, and even internal investigations within Central's ranks. Now, what was it to be?

"I'll help if I can," said Flint, knowing full well when he had said it that he somehow would soon be leaving the warmth and tranquility of Palos Verdes.

He could hear Harry breathe a sigh of relief, and then the deep voice sprang into action. "I've been involved in a lot of different things, Mike. Central has taken on more and more responsibility in the past three years or so, and we get mired in situations that get out of control at times." His voice now came over the phone in an uncharacteristically pleading tone. "Right now we have a hot one on our hands, and we need your help badly."

"Let me hear it all," said Flint. "If I can do anything, I'll assist you. Fair?"

"Look, Mike, we've got a twenty-four year old girl murdered," said Harry. "She was working for me, and Central, in a hush-hush way. We didn't think she was in any danger whatsoever, but now that she's dead, our entire operation could be in jeopardy."

"What do you mean by hush-hush?" asked Flint.

"She worked as an informer on street drugs," insisted Harry. "But no undercover stuff with mob types or hardcore sellers. We have a few dozen people on the streets just picking up bits and pieces of information, so that Central can get a handle on which direction the drug action is flowing. Again, I insist, this is low level information gathering."

Flint gave it some thought. "Why don't you turn it over to homicide?"

"That's our problem," said Harry. "It's out-of-town. We can't involve the local police."

"I don't understand," said Flint. "You said out-of-town. Where is that?"

"Saratoga," said Harry. "Little Old Saratoga."

"Now wait," said Flint. "Saratoga north or south?"

Harry gave a low laugh. "Where they run the ponies, Mike. You remember that place, don't you?"

"I remember it well, Harry. Very well."

And then, in his deep monologue, Harry continued to give the assorted, gruesome details of Robin's murder. Flint cocked one ear to the receiver and then slowly let it fall to his shoulder. Harry was spelling out everything, as was his habit when discussing Central's operations.

Flint's mind began to drift to another time in Saratoga. He remembered candlelight on small round tables and a cool summer's evening and the fragrance of the Spuyten Duyvil's primrose garden. The tingling sensation he got sitting across from a beautiful girl at their favorite table at the back of the garden, near the path where the yearling sales were conducted in August.

Men dressed smartly in custom-made shirts and suits, with hand-sewn ties and solid gold watches and tie pins. The trim, dark silk suits of the blue-bloods. And the Revlon faces of beautiful women. Tall, shapely. You could sit at that table and virtually smell the wealth, he remembered.

Everything seemed romantic in Saratoga that summer in 1970. It was a long, hot summer, and in the mornings they would drive to the lakes north of Saratoga and swim and boat until noon, before returning for the afternoon races at the famous track on Union Avenue.

In the evenings it was always an endless array of private parties. The big, sprawling mansions on Saratoga's upper Broadway were rented by those of great wealth and material success, and an invite here, and an invite there, added to the fascination and excitement of the season.

So there he was, among the beautiful people. A young man of 24. Young in age but not in experience. His right leg still healing from a wound he had received four years earlier in South Vietnam as a twenty-year-old Special Forces anti-guerrilla fighter, the leg still smarting from shrapnel fragments. The inexplicable *"Struggle in Southeast Asia"* as the press eventually labeled it was the war no one wanted to brag about; especially those in Saratoga in 1970.

The leg still held shrapnel fragments. So he kept his feelings about the war, and the details about his leg, to himself. The track and the people that gathered for it, was to be an immensely happy place. There could be no talk of Nam in this splendid, jubilant, August setting.

"It was an absolutely terrible way to die," he again was listening to Harry. "Someone held her head down in a tub. Can you imagine what that was like?"

Suddenly Flint's room in Palos Verdes seemed ten degrees cooler. It wasn't from fear. He had mastered that occupational neurosis long ago.

No matter how experienced he was--no matter how many times he had been involved with murder, the feeling was always the same. Almost melancholy, and too difficult to explain.

"And you don't have the slightest idea who might have done it?" asked Flint, holding back a yawn and eyeing the clock on his nightstand.

"Oh," replied Harry, mustering a second guess on the moment, "it might have been her ex-husband."

"So," insisted Flint, "find the husband and you've solved your problem."

"He could be any place," said Harry. "And if it isn't the husband, then we're right back to square one. She was reporting to us right along without any emotionalism, Mike. If she was having trouble with her ex, I'm certain she would have said something."

"I'm trying to figure how the husband knew her location. I thought you said it was a hush-hush operation?" asked Flint.

"That's what's got me puzzled," Harry said.

"O.K.," Flint interjected. "Let's say the husband did it. Let's at least pretend he killed her and departed Saratoga for places now unknown. Where does this leave the investigation with the Saratoga cops, State Police, or any other agency that might get involved?"

Harry had to think on this for a second before answering. "They may not be able to identify her right off," he finally said. "Yet even if they do identify her, there's nothing to link her to Central. At least no written communication. We do everything verbally. We use special lines, there will be no telephone company records to indicate incoming or outgoing calls to a particular location."

"Where are her nearest relatives?" Flint asked.

"She has a daughter." said Harry. Then, thinking about it, added, "The daughter, Sara, is staying with an aunt and uncle in Waycross, Georgia. It was an arrangement Robin made with them. She told me personally that she did not tell them what she was up to. She was more concerned that Sara had a nice home in which to live while she worked out her own problems. As for the local investigation, who knows. Sometimes they're followed up pretty thoroughly. Often they just put them on the back burner, along with other cases. I'm not so worried about the locals at this point, nor the State Police. I'm concerned that she might have talked to whoever killed her. There's always the possibility that one of the drug people discovered she was our informer. To tell you the truth, I'm at a loss on this one. That's why I need your expertise."

For some strange reason, Flint suddenly felt the urge to tell Harry he wasn't interested. He really didn't owe Harry any favors. And deep in his stomach he had that funny feeling that Harry was holding something back, though he decided for the moment not to press Harry any farther. It was evident Harry had a collapsing situation on his hands, self imposed or just circumstantial, but serious nevertheless. Flint fought off the temptation again to say no.

"I don't want to keep you on the phone for-ever," said Harry, "but I'd like to cover some of the happenings in the operation before this unfortunate incident. Can you give me a few more minutes?"

Flint concealed the boredom in his own voice, telling Harry to proceed.

"I've got to explain what we're doing upstate to begin with," Harry continued, the deep monologue and slow pace returning. "This drug scene has become so big, so widespread, it reaches everywhere. I told Central long ago, though they didn't listen, that it was getting too big, too far out-of-hand to be contained in New York City. Right now we know a lot of it is being directed from mob people in Canada. It's all connected to Montreal, Quebec and funnels its way down to New York. A good deal of it is upstate. That region around Saratoga is fairly affluent. Even the kids have lots of money to spend."

"Wait one minute," Flint snapped. "You're working out of Central's jurisdiction up there, aren't you?"

"I can't deny that," said Harry flatly.

"So," Flint added, "where does my backup come from if things go sour during my poking around?"

He heard Harry gurgle. Apparently the cigar saliva got caught in his throat, Flint figured. He waited while Harry cleared his pipes.

"God knows, Mike, but it's the reason I need you for the job. I can't have anyone getting caught up there. Least of all you."

"I'll need a lot of leeway if I decide to take this," Flint said. "And it isn't going to be easy on my own. Don't you have any reliable contacts I can work with in Saratoga?"

"Robin was all we had up there," replied Harry, a touch of nervousness detectable in his voice. "You'll be working blind. I can't offer any other assistance, except I will have one of my men meet and brief you as best he can when you get there. Of course, what he will show you will all be on paper, and much of it is second-hand information. I don't have much to work with. Robin was not the best communicator. But then, again, she was new at it."

"Anyway, as you were saying about the operation. Please continue." Flint coached him along.

And Harry, trying to collect his thoughts from the earlier interruption, began repeating some of what he had already said, at which Flint put the phone again on his shoulder and listened halfheartedly. In his thoughts, once more, Flint was back in Saratoga, entering the great ballroom of the *Canfield Casino* to attend a charity dance to benefit the National Racing Museum.

It was a sparkling crowd that warm summer evening, a mixture of Saratogians and visitors, including many of the rich, horsey set. A full tuxedoed orchestra was playing and to add atmosphere to the affair, they were parking cars in an outer parking lot and transporting guests to the dance in horse-drawn carriages.

It was then he noticed the terribly attractive dark-haired girl in the orange and black Italian print dress, escorted into the ballroom on the arm of an older, yet handsome white-haired man. He followed her movement about the room for part of the night, and later when going to the bar for a drink, she came in his direction and he came face to face with her strikingly blue eyes.

There seemed to be an immediate surge of electricity between them at this first encounter. He felt it instantly.

A glance again in her direction. A nod with the head as she sat with her escort, and a nod in reply. Then music, and he found himself coming to her table, as if drawn by a magnetic force, finding that he was compelled to ask her to dance.

Alice Winslow Holmes, femininity, class, background, old money, with her long dark flowing hair and schoolgirl-like silhouette, dancing as if on air bubbles with Mike Flint across the Casino's ballroom floor to string music. While her escort, none other than her father, looked on with smiling approval. But with his bad leg, Flint couldn't keep up with her, and when he begged her to sit down, she moved to the side of the dance floor and slowed her movements to accommodate him.

It was a wondrous night. He delighted in her newfound company, enjoying every moment with her. She was full of unlimited energy, and her eyes, as blue as he could ever remember seeing on anyone, glistened with merriment.

Yes, he had found an absolutely beautiful creature, in a setting befit for a king.

"Isn't it wonderful?" she had said laughingly,

surveying the room leisurely and to her father, saying, "I'd like you to meet Mike Flint, Dad," and her father, asking, "And where are you from lad, what do you do?"

"That's not important tonight," Alice was quick to say, taking Flint's arm. "Let us dance and enjoy ourselves. We can spend time at lunch talking of such things. Can't we, Mike Flint?"

Their meeting was as simple and as effortless as that. Flint was in his last year of college, finishing up on the G.I. bill, with plans to attend law school if his money held out, and he had the brains to withstand law school's rigid academic demands.

Alice had graduated from Smith College and was employed by her uncle who owned a chain of large hotels. Her position was not exactly defined, though she later told Flint it was nothing more than putting in time in big offices in Boston to give her some career identity.

In the short span of two weeks after meeting Alice, Flint seemingly went everywhere in Saratoga with her. They would sit in her family box at the track and watch every race, betting a few dollars here and there on horses known to her father and placing ten or twenty on the nose when one of her father's horses ran. Holmes was not a big thoroughbred owner, but he did maintain at least four horses himself and had money invested with others in about a dozen more.

Alice said it had been a favorite family hobby since her great-great grandfather Holmes's time.

In the evenings it was off to dine in a variety of places. One of his special delights was Siro's near the track where, after dinner, they would gather about the piano bar and sing songs. Or sit outside under Siro's tent and sip gin and tonics and enjoy the cool summer night's air, he taking her hands in his and becoming almost hypnotized with her loveliness.

Flint was not given to believing in premonitions. But he felt, at times when with Alice, that all that was happening to them that summer was too real to be true and couldn't possibly last.

They just about ran the full gamut of Saratoga's summer social events, and had met most of the racing elite. Flint was very impressed with this group and though he felt uneasy at first when making their acquaintance, Alice was always close by and often came to his rescue on seemingly momentary cue.

Alice didn't talk much about her mother at first, though she was fond of talking about her father. "No," she said when he asked where her mother was, "she decided not to attend the races this season. She's been suffering from congestive heart problems for the past three years. Saratoga has been ruled out by her doctor."

Her father, Harris Holmes, was very proper and extremely polite on all the occasions Flint and Alice were in his company, starting from the minute Flint was introduced to him at the *Canfield Casino* following Flint's first dance with Alice.

Yet Flint found him, at times, emotionally subdued, whereas Alice was feverishly active and natural in all her charming ways.

There was one moment when Harris Holmes let his feelings about his daughter appropriately known to Flint. It came in the third week of their relationship, and it was more of a statement of open and spontaneous admiration, and not a response to any inquiry from Flint, though Flint had intended to discuss Alice with her father at some point along the way.

They had just come from the annual yearling sales where, Flint had witnessed, to his amazement, Harris Holmes sign his name to a letter of credit for a cool three hundred fifty thousand dollars, sealing Holmes's successful bid on a great chestnut colt. It was all done in the wink of an eye. The bidding had gone on for a full five minutes and there were several others who stayed with Holmes from the first upset price of seventy-five thousand. It was narrowed to three bidders when the price went over three hundred thousand. Holmes wanted this horse very much. He later said he was willing to go to four hundred thousand if necessary.

To celebrate his purchase, Holmes invited some buyers and Flint for a glass of a magnificent vintage French champagne. It was to be a man's celebration; the women, including Alice and some of her friends, had long since gone home for the evening. The men were to get down to some serious and skillful champagne drinking, a ritual at most yearling sales gatherings.

They assembled at the bar near the sales pavilion. Two gleaming silver ice buckets were already awaiting them. The champagne, upon earlier instructions from the head bartender, had been chilled.

Holmes, beaming and laughing, lifted one of the bottles in an appropriate gesture and proceeded to pop the cork.

"Gentlemen," he said, pointing the bottle away from everyone at an angle, "this is a rare 1952 vintage. It's to be sipped, not guzzled," at which they all broke out in loud laughter.

So as they drank of the expensive effervescence, several toasts to Holmes and his colt were given. It was a special night, Flint remembered, it was also the last time he would see Harris Holmes alive, though in the cool Saratoga evening air in this time of celebration, not a soul would have guessed it. When the last of five such vintage bottles were depleted, Flint found himself lingering at the bar, a bit tipsy, alone with Harris Holmes. There were still many people about the sales area, though the lights were mostly turned down except those at the bar itself.

"I want to walk over and see my colt," said Holmes in a friendly way to Flint. "It's late, I know, but I have a strong feeling that horse and I have a destiny. I think...I believe, he has the bloodlines in him to be a big stakes winner. I really believe that."

They strolled slowly to barn seven where the colt was standing, his head lifted high and proud above the heavy stall door. The colt jumped back quickly as they approached the stall.

"Ah. You see," exclaimed Holmes, "this fellow has a fine pedigree."

"And very spirited," Flint added.

"He's a class animal. We're going to win a lot of races big fellow, aren't we?"

The colt blew a stream of hot breath from his nostrils and the vapor was like a thick mist in the night's chilled air.

Holmes rested one hand on Flint's left shoulder as they walked slowly back toward the pavilion.

"Alice is very special to me," Holmes said languidly to Flint. "Mrs. Holmes has not been well for some time and it has put undue pressure on Alice, I'm sure. Still, through it all, Alice hasn't complained. She has been my strength, also."

"I agree," Flint said meditatively, suddenly thinking about her and being reinvaded by her beauty.

"My daughter was very quiet," Holmes went on. "Until this year she has kept pretty much to herself. I'm glad you have been able to bring her out of her shell. It's been good for her."

Holmes was wearing thick-rimmed glasses which kept slipping down on his nose, so he decided to take them off. He also felt somewhat wobbly from the champagne. They slowed their pace and Flint, noticing that he was partly drunk, cupped one hand under Holmes's elbow and guided him back along the narrow walk to the bar.

"We will have a nightcap," Holmes said to the bartender. "Make mine beer. And what will you have Flint?"

"Beer also."

"Two beers it will be," said the bartender.

They were both stirred by the awareness that for the first time they were talking quite freely and frankly.

"I'm not prone to bragging," Holmes continued, turning to look at Flint, "but Alice is a very smart girl. An extraordinary girl. She graduated cum laude from Smith College. Did you know that?"

"No, I didn't," said Flint truthfully, looking at Holmes and noticing how perfectly he personified the rich, New England born, Presbyterian gentleman. The gleaming, thick white hair and the narrow, heavily tanned face of a man who, though native to Boston, Massachusetts, spent most of the winters now in Florida and California.

"My only dream these days is to see that Alice is happy. Can you understand that, Flint?" Holmes was staring at him now, his glasses still in his hands. His eyes were wide open, and he paused, as if waiting for Flint to again agree with him.

"She is happy," Flint said. "She's wonderfully happy, I can assure you."

Holmes now beamed at him. "I really believe she has found someone she can be happy with. I first thought this sudden flirtation was all nonsense with you and Alice. I now see it is taking

31

hold of you both. I'm prayerful it will not fade with the season."

"I don't think it will, Mr. Holmes," said Flint. "As you say, Alice is a very special person. She is quite exceptional."

"I'm glad to hear you say it," Holmes said, now with his glasses back on, smiling admiringly at Flint. "Now let's go home and sleep off this drink and we'll meet for lunch tomorrow. That is, if you can make it."

They left the pavilion bar just as the last lights were being turned out. As they walked to Holmes's chauffeur-driven limousine, he stopped and looked once more at the barn where the great chestnut colt was housed.

"You know," Holmes said in a tone of pleasure, "I believe I've bought a real champion."

Then Flint was aware again of Harry's booming voice, and he lifted the receiver once again to his ear. "I'm sorry, what were you saying, Harry?"

" My god, Flint. Haven't you been listening to anything? I know it's late, but this is top priority," Harry pleaded. Then he was off in a new flurry of details about Robin's murder.

"Give me one moment," said Flint. "I want to tape this, so I can go over it again in the morning."

Flint hit a button near his phone and immediately Harry could hear a soft, scratching noise. "It's recording, Harry. Please continue," said Flint, moving the receiver to his shoulder once more, listening in utter silence.

He then searched his memory for more coherent recollection of his few summer weeks with Alice and her father. He recalled vividly the day everything changed, and a sudden blackness invaded the balmy tranquility of that August.

A call came to his apartment on Church Street shortly before noon about a week later, as he was preparing to leave for the track to meet Alice. It was from Charles Hudson, a close friend of the Holmeses.

"Mr. Flint," Hudson said in low, unsteady voice, "I have some sad news for you. Very sad indeed...."

Flint's first thought was that something had happened to Alice and, as he held the phone, his mind started drawing irrational conclusions and his heart began to beat quickly and blood swelled in his temples.

His previous premonition flashed across his thoughts.

He paused, captured his composure, and delicately asked Hudson the dreaded question, "Has something happened to Alice?"

"Oh, I'm sorry," Hudson said, realizing that had alarmed Flint greatly. "Alice is fine."

"Then what is it?" asked Flint.

"Harris Holmes has been killed," Hudson said, his voice clearly betraying an underlying sadness.

Flint was silent for a moment. He felt his throat go dry as the shock of the statement gripped his whole body. Then his concern turned immediately to Alice. "Where is Alice?" he heard himself asking Hudson.

"That's the reason I'm calling," said Hudson. "She's on her way to Boston to be with her mother. The dreadful irony of all this is that it was her mother who they all worried about. The entire affair is a nightmare. I still can't believe it happened."

It then dawned on Flint that Hudson hadn't said what actually happened to Harris Holmes. "You said Harris was killed," Flint said. "Where, when did this happen?"

He waited for a reply, and after a moment Hudson said, "They found Harris with the colt. He apparently was squeezed against the stall of the barn and died from internal bleeding. He went to the barn sometime before sunrise. We don't know why he went at that hour. The night watchman said he heard nothing. The colt must have been startled or something. It's the most unfortunate accident. It's terrible."

Flint made arrangements to go directly to Boston where, he had been told by Hudson, Holmes's funeral and interment would take place.

Upon his arrival, he went to the Holmes residence to see Alice. He was met at the door by a housemaid who greeted him with almost grim indifference.

"Alice can not be seen at this time," said the maid, holding the door half closed to Flint as she spoke. He would have to call by phone later, perhaps. No outsiders would attend the funeral. The family burial would be private.

His phone call the following day went unanswered. He sent a note, which also was not acknowledged. He stayed on in Boston for a week, trying desperately to understand why Alice was shutting him out of her life. He read in the *Boston Globe* that the private funeral had taken place two days after his arrival. More attempts were made to contact Alice, including, in his desperation to get through to her, a teletype message. He eventually gave up trying and left Boston. The bitterness and bewilderment of the situation haunted him for weeks.

Some four months later, quite unexpectedly, while he was living in New York City trying desperately to get over Alice, he received a letter from Alice. Its sudden appearance stunned him. It had no return address, but he did notice it was postmarked Palm Beach, Florida.

It was brief and rather somber, yet obviously in Alice's handwriting, with her familiar flowing large letters.

Dear Mike,

There is no way to explain what happened in Boston. You will have to accept it for what it was. Now that father is gone I must devote my-self completely to my ailing mother. I hope you will understand.

Love, Alice.

It was the last correspondence he ever had with her.

"It's touchy, Flint," Harry repeated. "I can't tell you enough how important this is."

Flint was about to hang up, then hesitated, adding, "One thing must be understood, Harry. I like a free hand in these situations. If you or anyone else starts to put restrictions on me, I'll call the whole thing off...agreed?"

"I'll notify everyone to stay clear," said Harry. "Remember, it could be a political problem as well if the locals catch on."

"O.K.," Flint concluded, "but let me handle the local situation. By the way, make sure your man brings along some cash. I'm not doing anything without an advance."

There was a long pause. Then Harry, in a more somber tone, said, "Thanks, Mike. This means a lot to me."

Flint heard the receiver click down at Harry's end. He went to the dresser and opened a fresh pack of cigarettes, staring into the small mirror on the wall as he lit one.

He suddenly realized that he didn't have a nice face anymore. The years had somehow etched the skin and he now appeared hard. He would be forty-two in six weeks. Unlike many men his age, his hair wasn't affected by the years.Thick and curly, it remained black, even around the sideburns. The change was most no-ticeable near the eyes. The pale outline of an old scar over his right cheekbone had become more conspicuous. He had no admiration for what he saw in the mirror.

"Awful," he thought. There wasn't the faintest touch of joy in that face.

He'd called his own shots for several years now, and he made a great deal of money, but this line of work was getting to him and he knew it. If things had gone just a bit differently after college, if he had gone on to law school, if things had worked out better that summer at Sarratoga... There were a lot of ifs along the way that might have changed his life.

But the years had a way of slipping by. His life during those years had been like a blitz. Three years as a detective on a major city police force. Five years with Army Intelligence. Three years with the CIA. He might have stayed with the CIA had it not been for a personal conflict with his immediate superior, Ed Bailey, a bastard if ever he met one.

So, fed up one day with all of it, he decided to branch out on his own. He had the experience and the contacts. He knew every chiseler and crook on the East and West coasts, not to mention his international contacts. Capitalizing on this knowledge, he let it be known he was a free agent.

There were a few lean times at first, waiting for work, but eventually work came his way. He soon had more assignments than he could handle.

The work had some compensations that suited his lifestyle as well -- the most attractive being lots of time off between jobs.

He thought for a moment about Harry's phone call. He really didn't have to take this one. His debts to Harry had long since been paid in full. If anything, Harry owed him a favor.

The weather in southern California was perfect this February. He had no set plans, but still there were things he wanted to do. He was part owner of a sloop, now moored at Marina Del Rey. He'd only been out on it twice in six months. Some friends were planning a trip to Mexico. He was invited. He wanted to do it all. Harry's call started that weird stirring in his blood which always told him his work would take precedence.

He put out the cigarette and went back to bed. When he woke it was past noon and a warm breeze was blowing through the bedroom window. After a while, he called the airlines and made his reservation.

Upon checking his watch he noticed he was five minutes late for his date. It was a rarity for Flint, for he always prided himself on being punctual.

He showered, dressed, and left his apartment within fifteen minutes. California was hot, even for February, but Flint still felt a slight chill. "My imagination," he said to himself. He shrugged his shoulders and continued on.

3. Georgio, Isn't It?

On the flight from Los Angeles to Chicago, Flint dozed off, waking only when he heard the nasal voice of the flight attendant announcing that they would be landing within seven or so minutes and that the captain was requesting everyone to fasten their seat belts.

It was still daylight and they expected the stopover time to be no more than forty minutes. He would be switching planes for the final run to Albany. At O'Hare Airport he grabbed a drink and killed time reading a local paper.

A big, new winter storm was moving west to east, so the paper read, but for now the weather was perfect and sunny, with temperatures in the mid-thirties.

After a few minutes he set the newspaper down and pulled a small leather notebook from his coat pocket and began reading the information Harry had phoned to him. Information he had written down along with taping Harry's conversation.

He studied the notes, stopping at a point where Harry had said, in effect, that his snitch, Robin, was a low key informer. Then continued reading and stopped once again where he had circled five other words "it might have been anyone."

This made no sense to Flint. What did Harry

mean by anyone? Was he making light of their conversation, or was he of the opinion that it really was someone other than her husband?

He then put the notebook back in his pocket and hurried to catch the Albany flight, pondering as he went, what Saratoga might be like now, having not been there for so many years.

As the American Airline jet made its approach to the Albany Airport two hours later, seemingly tilting as it turned, Flint, sitting on a window seat, could plainly see the runway. It dawned on him that this was a mere postage stamp of a landing strip compared to the large airports he'd become accustomed to in his travels about the world.

It was now late afternoon and the ground below, except for the airstrip and the roads leading to and from the airport, was a vast white blanket of snow, and he immediately disliked its appearance.

He cursed Harry silently for summoning him to this cold, wintry place.

The plane was down on the runway safely now, taxiing to the long, low terminal building which was well lighted from within with large windows. The lights shone through the windows and he could see swirls of snow blowing across the open tarmac. It wasn't actually snowing. The strong gusts, however, gave it the appearance of falling snow. As they came closer to the building, the wind gusts were picking up velocity and you could feel its pressure against the plane as it came to a stop, its engine winding down, as if groaning against the cold.

A blast of frigid air whipped at his face as he stepped gingerly down the plane's steps. On the ten-yard dash to the terminal building, the sudden deep biting cold penetrated his unlined trench coat, went straight through a mid-weight wool sweater he was wearing underneath, and chilled his entire body.

He was glad to be inside the terminal building with its comforting heat. Passengers were moving about, being greeted by relatives, business associates, or just friends, and amid the clamor of voices, Flint kept a diligent eye out for Harry's man, though he wasn't certain who that person would be.

Five minutes passed and all of the departing passengers were just about cleared of the area. Flint waited about anxiously, but no one showed up. With the exception of one airline ticket agent at the small receiving counter and two elderly ladies sitting near the exit door, the area was empty. He gave it two more minutes. Then, wearily, he trudged the hundred or so yards to the baggage claim section and gathered up his things.

He then shuffled to a nearby pay phone, carrying a night bag over his right shoulder and a suitcase in each hand. He set the luggage down and proceeded to dial Harry's special number in New York City, a coded number given to a few select individuals. He was about to reach for the first code number when a figure stepped smartly around from the other side of the four-unit phone stand and touched his dialing arm.

Flint turned quickly, dropping his arm as he spun to one side. He saw half a man's face. The other half was hidden up under a snap-brimmed, soft-gray felt fedora. Below the brim, he looked at a dark mustache and a finely chiseled chin. Flint immediately recognized the profile and called out, "Georgio . . . It is Georgio, isn't it?" Flint watched the chin drop open and a full set of gleaming white teeth showed in a full smile.

"You have a wonderful memory, Flint. You remember old Georgio. Harry said, don't say a word to him. See if he remembers. After all these years, see if he can remember you. See if his brain is still alert. That's what Harry said."

"I never forget a face," said Flint, looking Georgio over closely as if to make absolutely certain he was right. "I haven't gone soft in the head. Not yet. You can tell that to Harry when you next see him."

Georgio was wearing a dark blue, full-length cashmere overcoat which was unbuttoned. Flint noticed that underneath, Georgio wore a neatly pressed gray pin-striped suit, just a shade darker than his fedora. He also wore an expensive light blue silk tie. He looked more like an investment banker than a cop, Flint thought.

Flint eyed him up and down once more, then spoke again. "Night comes early in these parts, doesn't it?"

"Na. Na." replied Georgio, pointing to the large terminal windows with the snow still flying past it like clouds of smoke. "It's still daylight. It only looks like night because of the snow. We still have about one hour of daylight. You're too used to California. They tell me the sun shines all the time in L.A." His teeth showed white again under his mustache.

"Maybe I should have stayed in California," said Flint. "In fact, Chicago was warmer than here."

During all the small talk, Flint was sizing Georgio up. He figured the coat made Georgio look larger than he actually was. But he guessed that Georgio weighed about 190 and stood about five-foot-eleven inches, minus the fedora. He held his age well, Flint noticed. He could be in his late fifties, but he could easily pass for early or mid-fifties. The face did not show wrinkles either at the eyes or around the lower mouth. He appeared to Flint very much as he had remembered him in the old days.

Flint couldn't help but notice Georgio's hands. They were quite stubby, though well manicured. A point Flint observed with amused interest.

A very well dressed, well manicured cop. What was New York's finest coming to? Even the cops were going Wall Street.

"One thing I'd like to know right off," Flint asked. "Am I strictly working on this case alone, or has Harry decided to give me some back-up?"

Georgio shifted his hands so that they now crossed over his chest and Flint caught a glimpse of two gold rings, one with a nice diamond set, that he hadn't really noticed before.

"You're it," Georgio was quick to answer. "I'm to take you to Saratoga, fill you in on where things were and now stand, and then I'm out of these parts. I've got duties in New York. I'm sorry, but that's the way Harry left it."

"Harry knows I always work alone," added Flint. "We've had this understanding. I want to go it alone on this one. But back-up is something different. Who's been directing the network in this region? Who did Robin network with up here?"

Georgio gave him a puzzled look. "This was not one of our normal operations," he said. "Didn't Harry tell you that?"

"He filled me in pretty well," said Flint.

"Then you have it as it is, there ain't much else to say. We have moved out in the past few years. It was a necessity. The information in the city doesn't come through as it used to. You can't rely on your best snitch these days. We have a good handle on where the drugs are moving. Harry and Central thought if they could telegraph the moves, at least those heading for the city,... well, maybe we could stop a major portion of it.

These druggies talk a lot. Robin wasn't anyone specially trained. All she had to do was listen on the streets of Saratoga, maybe mingle with the drug types. They always seem to have information on movements of that nature."

Flint stared at Georgio for a moment. The idea of using an amateur such as Robin to gather this type of information suddenly seemed preposterous to him.

"You know, Georgio," he finally said with some disgust in his voice, "this whole thing smells rotten. Really rotten."

Georgio's stubby hand turned in front of Flint and, pulling up his sleeve, he displayed a solid-gold watch.

"Hey, it's getting late," Georgio changed the subject. "We'd better get started."

They lifted Flint's bags and went out the sliding doors to the parking area, blowing, cold snow following them as they went. Georgio flipped open the trunk of a large, black-colored Olds sedan, hurriedly loaded in Flint's belongings, and within five minutes they were out of the parking lot of Albany Airport, driving south along the tail end of the runway toward Interstate 87, the super highway that would lead them to Saratoga, some 30 miles north of the airport.

As they made a sharp left swing to the approach ramp to I-87, a large gray building loomed up through the snowy mist. Flint read the sign under two big floodlights, *"Capital Land Newspapers."* Georgio was staring straight ahead as the car entered the three-lane I-87, and Flint felt the speed increase and whiffs of curling snow, kicked up by the cars in front made it necessary to turn on the windshield wipers.

"We're in a helluva mess," Georgio confided to Flint. "We can't stop the stuff from coming into the city and we can't pinpoint the sources, either. We're supposed to be the elite professional branch of the police forces, but the situation is getting worse day by day."

"Don't feel bad," Flint replied. "This is only the beginning. I saw a lot of this dope in Central America ten years ago. I also saw it in the Middle East, in China, Burma and elsewhere. Now that they've found a market that will pay hard cash to get it, it's open season on the United States. Hell, they can get one hundred times more for heroin and cocaine here than they can anywhere in the Far East."

"Yeah." said Georgio. "It's big money. We caught this kid in Queens last year. He had fifty-five thousand dollars worth of cocaine in his small garret apartment. He was a page at the United Nations making three hundred a week, but we later discovered he was clearing another six hundred a week for simply storing the stuff for three street peddlers." He turned to face Flint and his chin lifted and the white teeth showed again. "This kid also was hooked into two other guys in the U.N. We made a move on them. You know what happened?" He drew in a breath and hissed it out again. "I'll tell you what happened. Nothing. They both had diplomatic immunity. Two punks, making a ton of bread selling cocaine. We couldn't do a thing about it. That's what we're up against."

Flint rubbed his hand on the side window and peered out again at the landscape. The gray snowy afternoon was now beginning to turn dark. He remained quiet for a spell. He was still giving second thoughts as to why he had accepted this assignment. And why, thinking further about it, should Harry have called him in on such a cut-and-dried murder? He couldn't fully under-stand Harry's reasoning on this one. Unless, of course, Harry knew the whole episode had nothing to do with the husband to begin with. He was giving it some very serious thought when Georgio inquired, as if reading his mind, "I bet you wish you didn't come East, Flint."

"It's a little late for that," Flint replied. "But you're right. I'm not sure Harry needs me for this job. If it's her husband, then let the local cops handle it. We can save our cloak-and-dagger stuff for more important things."

"Harry's a dumb bastard at times," Georgio said. His expression didn't change as he said it. It was a statement that just seemed to come out naturally, but Flint was taken by surprise. He knew that Georgio had worked with Harry since the early sixties and there had always been, at least to the best of Flint's observation, a mutual admiration among the two. It was strange to hear Georgio admonish Harry.

Georgio had handed Flint an envelope containing background information on Robin, bits and pieces of info on what she had been reporting to Central during her brief period in Saratoga and comments penciled in by Harry and what he thought of the various internal data.

Flint read them as the car moved further northward, with Georgio now concentrating on his driving and remaining silent. As had become his habit, Flint read each line, pausing for a moment between each to lock the information into his memory. In his business, it had become essential to develop a good memory. Written information was considered very risky to carry around on one's person. Trusting important data to memory was always safer in Flint's line of work.

Flint set the papers he had been reading on his lap. Then, turning to Georgio, he said, "I'd like to hear what you've heard so far concerning Robin's murder."

Georgio turned to face him, and his teeth

showed white again and his nose wrinkled up above his mustache. "I'm not sure of everything they say at Central," he replied. "They, meaning Harry and others, say it's all dope related. Up-state peddlers, supposedly coming from Quebec City. But we don't have a handle on just how heavy the traffic is, nor who's directing the operation." His head kept turning to Flint and then back to the road as he spoke. "About the kid's murder. I can't say. Who can? Someone got to her, somehow. But you never know about these things. She might have been killed for another reason. You got Harry's thinking on it. It's anybody's guess what really happened."

Flint reached in his upper right pocket and took out a cigarette, pushed in the car lighter and lit it. He puffed slowly, letting out a long breath of smoke, at which Georgio touched the electric window button and dropped Flint's window about a full inch to help dissipate the smoke that was quickly accumulating.

"If it's too cold, let me know," he qualified his action with a smile.

Flint picked up the papers and resumed reading them. The small trail of smoke from his cigarette now funneled its way out the window opening.

There really wasn't much substance in Robin's reports. It was a bunch of little things, often repeated, and very amateurish at best. For example, Flint read with repetitive boredom Robin's last three reports, each one coming into to Central by phone and then transcribed by one of the special typists.

"Slow day. Someone said there was a fresh shipment of crack. I could not find where it was coming from nor who was handling it. There's a guy named Pinky who usually gets it for the kids at the college, but he's not the main pusher.

There are others about town. Someone said there's a man that lives on a big boat over in Schuylerville about a half hour from here that sells dope in the summer months. I have no idea where he goes in the winter."

Robin's recurring theme throughout her reports pointed to "slow" uneventful happenings. The more he read, the more Flint became infuriated with Harry for having hired such a young, inexperienced girl. Then, turning to Georgio once more, he said in a tone of regret, "Did she ever once come up with any useful information?"

"I'm afraid not," replied Georgio. "She really was of no use. I think Harry kept her on the payroll out of sympathy. As an informer, she was a dud."

Flint thought about it for a moment. In his mind he was now trying to piece it together. It appeared on the surface that it was going to be a hopeless task. What information he had was of little use. He would have to develop some pattern to Robin's movements and whereabouts in the days and nights just before her death in order to even begin to get close to what really happened. He knew that it would be a painstakingly slow process gathering this information on her.

Flint would have to start consolidating his own facts. He would be in Saratoga, living incognito. Nevertheless, he would have to have communication with persons in and about the area if he were to find what led to Robin's death. Better yet, what was it that she knew that caused her death? His instincts told him that she was killed because she knew something of great importance. Whether it was about the dope traffic or something else, he would have to sort it out.

Georgio was muttering something out of the corner of his mouth about the damnable cold weather, and as they drove north, the gray afternoon, with snow still swirling in all directions, was suddenly turning dark.

Flint checked his watch. It was exactly 5 p.m. Could it be possible, Flint was thinking, that all this was happening in little ol' Saratoga? He could see lights now and then, from homes along the Northway, though most of them were set quite a distance from the road. The ride was fairly flat, though the car did encounter some dips, and at one point there was a long steady decline and then a long uphill climb. They had crossed a rather expansive bridge with a valley running beneath, and at this point Flint could make out sparks of brilliant color far off, lights he assumed from some town or small hamlet.

"What did she do with her spare time?" Flint found himself asking Georgio. "Did she have any hobbies, special interests. Anything that we might go on in that direction?"

Georgio turned, and his eyes widened. "Precisely the question I asked Harry. He didn't know a thing about her activities. I'm not saying Central is totally unsympathetic with all the snitches it hires. But in this case, I just can't say."

Flint's lips pursed in a silent whistle of disgust. Then he said, "I've taken particular note of the lack of her profile in this report." His hands fumbled the papers once again. "It would appear, at least from my judgment, that things are getting pretty sloppy at Central. Is that the case?"

"Sloppy," Georgio replied quietly. "Perhaps not sloppy. I call it more confused than sloppy. You have to know where we're coming from these days, Flint. We've got more work than we can properly handle. We're understaffed. Budgets have been cut. We haven't the time to screen everyone. We used to in the old days. No one would be hired unless we had their entire history, including that of their parents and relatives. We used to be more thorough with our background investigations. We were more thorough than the Feds at one time. Today, unfortunately, you take what you can get. It's not nice, but it's the truth."

Flint couldn't accept it. He could not reason why they hired people with no experience. Budget or no budget. So he picked the papers up once again and read on. It was not the detailed, exacting reports he was used to reading. But he knew that somewhere among all those bland sentences, Robin was trying to say something of importance, though it was difficult, if not impossible at this juncture, to pinpoint.

He noticed a quick reference Robin made about a certain person named Benson. She did not give the first name. Flint was not certain it was male or female. He assumed, and it was strictly a guess, that this Benson was a local contact of some importance to Robin, though she didn't elaborate nor spell out the relationship. There was a continued, vague description to all her reports. Flint deemed from them that she was bored with what she was doing for Central, and that these reports, though demanded by Central, were delivered out of duress.

It was another piece of information that Flint would tuck away in his memory. Almost unconsciously, be began the mental process of consolidating her person in his mind, methodically drawing an inner picture of Robin's physical and psychological makeup. Through his years of training, he had been taught to recognize a person's strengths and weaknesses by the way they expressed themselves in writing. He could ascertain these same conclusions by verbal communication, also.

He detected a concurrent carelessness to Robin's personality. A hesitancy and nervousness that permeated her reports. So much so, that it was irritating to read them.

He could read no more. He set the papers down and glanced once more at Georgio, whose eyes were glued to the snowy road, his paunchy chin half hidden in his neck, as he leaned forward near the steering wheel like a race driver.

"How much further?" he asked with a disinterested yawn. Georgio's head snapped back, as if startled from a trance.

"We can't be far from the exit," he said. "It's Exit 13. Keep your eyes peeled for the sign."

They drove under another overpass, then the highway ran flat for about three miles or so. Eventually Georgio spotted the Exit 13 sign, even though it was half covered with snow.

They turned into a long, circling exit which brought them right back over the highway, and pointed the car in a westerly direction. For the first time since they had departed Albany Airport, Georgio eased up on the gas and seemed to relax.

The snow swirls were subsiding, and as the car mounted a hilly section, the road divided and Flint noticed a long line of glittering street lamps.

Then Georgio, swinging his head to the left, shouted out, "That's the track over there."

Flint could make out a tall iron fence, but nothing more. Yet, as they drove further, the great elephantine structure's outline came into view; though it was merely a gray silhouette against the winter night sky.

How barren it looks now, he thought to himself. How ghost-like.

"Harry's got a neat little place for you, Flint." Georgio said. "He thought first about putting you up in the downtown section. But then he had second thoughts, especially since Robin lived downtown." He turned to Flint and smiled. "You'll be holing up in one of the big mansions near the track. Harry feels it's safer and besides, it's only a mile or so from the downtown area."

As he was speaking, Georgio turned into a wide driveway which extended for about fifty yards. It was tree-lined on both sides. The driveway ended in a cul-de-sac and, looming before them in the headlight's glare, Flint got his first glimpse of his temporary home in Saratoga. A large, three-story Dutch Renaissance type mansion, with double wide oak doors and a large pillared porch, one of the prized relics of Saratoga's golden era. A sumptuous home no doubt of some long forgotten millionaire, the great mansion was now unoccupied, its historical presence weathering out another cold northern winter in silence.

Georgio then cranked the wheel sharply to the right, pulling in along the side of the mansion. He shut off the car and leaned back against the seat and let out a relieved sigh.

"This is it," he said with a small laugh. "You're home, Flint. Like it or not."

Flint didn't say anything. He listened instead to the wind and snow pelting on the car. He was of a mind to tell Georgio to forget it all, but he kept his thoughts inside.

Then, finally he spoke. "Well, let's unload this heap." The minute Flint opened the door, the temperature dropped some 50 degrees. It was bitter cold and his hands were freezing even before he was able to grab his first piece of luggage and haul it to the side door which Georgio had already opened.

It took three quick trips to get everything out of the car. Once inside, they shut the door and stood in the near pitch darkness, catching their breath and warming their hands by clapping them together.

"Hell," Flint cursed. "It's damn cold in here,

too. "Harry was worried about you, you know," Georgio said. "He said if anything gets to Flint, it will be the cold weather. I think he was right."

"When you see Harry, tell him my fee just went up. Will you do that for me?" Flint barked.

By this time Georgio was working his way through the dark to the rear of the large room with the help of a small pocket flashlight. He kept it faced to the floor and Flint watched, with some amusement, as Georgio struggled with the largest piece of luggage as he tried to negotiate through a door with the piece turned sideways.

Georgio, apparently out of shape, was laboring in his breathing, Flint noticed.

At the head of the stairs, Georgio opened another door and entered a small apartment which was already lighted. It consisted of four rooms, a bath and small kitchen. It was simply furnished, yet warm and comfortable.

"This is Central's safe house in Saratoga," said Georgio, setting down Flint's largest suitcase. "When you come up the stairs, the lights are activated automatically by an electric eye. It's the only way up here, so should someone other than yourself come up those stairs during the night, you'll have plenty of warning by the lights." He smiled at Flint. "However, I don't think you'll have unexpected guests. We've had this place for at least eight years now, and it's proven itself safe."

"What about fire?" Flint asked. "Where do I go?"

Georgio pointed to dark curtains covering sets of windows in each of the rooms. "You open them and jump. Hell, it's only two stories."

Flint went to the drapes, but Georgio pulled him by the arm. "Please. Please don't open them now. I assure you, there's windows there. You can't see any light with these special drapes from the outside. This house is considered vacant by everyone up here. Harry says you can stay where you want. A hotel perhaps in town. Or a motel on the outskirts. You're not restricted to this place. It's really for your protection, just in case . . ."

"Just in case of what?" Flint interrupted.

"One never knows," replied Georgio.

Flint began unpacking as he was talking. Georgio sat on the edge of a small couch in the room they had first entered. His short legs dangling but not quite touching the soft brownish colored wall-to-wall carpet.

Then Georgio went to the kitchen and placed a large piece of paper on the counter which he had taken from his inside pocket. "You're obviously wondering where we're located. Let me show you." He quickly drew a double line, indicating the Northway they had just come off, then the route past the track to the mansion. He then drew several squares, showing surrounding structures and another line, which to Flint appeared to be a street between the houses to the rear of the mansion.

"This whole neighborhood of big homes has been sitting idle for several years," Georgio continued. "It was a proposed extension of the track grounds, but they haven't come up with the money to go ahead with the project. There are eight homes in a row in back of this one that are vacant, and five on either side that are vacant. There's a 15-acre wooded lot across the road that's tied into the extension project. So, as you can see, the place is quite secluded."

Flint looked down at the scribbling and pondered it for a moment.

"I'm safe but remote," Flint finally said. "What do I do for transportation?"

"You have several options," said Georgio, standing up straight, the incredible pinky ring shining even more luminously under the kitchen's overhead light. "If you go out the back way, it's but a short walk to the next side street. One block down to the right there's a small all-night gas station. They serve coffee and some foodstuffs. You can usually catch a cab from this location. The cabbies hang around this station day and night waiting for their dispatchers to call. It's also a good drop off point, because you can come and go from there and no one will know exactly where to."

"It sounds inconvenient," Flint reasoned. "Besides, I'll freeze my butt off walking there."

Georgio threw up his hands. "I'm only telling you the options."

"Continue," said Flint.

"Two houses down there's a big carriage house. It's got three wide, tall wooden doors. We have a car stored there for you. The driveway from the carriage house is linked to the house in the rear. You can drive straight out. Take a sharp left and you'll be headed for downtown Saratoga." He paused to draw the driveway on the paper. "You see," he continued. "It's less than 100 yards to the street. But I have to caution you, you could draw attention to yourself should someone spot the car lights."

Flint laughed. "You said the whole neighborhood is vacant."

"True. It is," said Georgio. "But who's to say at a given time, that someone might not be passing by and see you. Kids roaming, lovers seeking seclusion. Again, it's only a word to the wise. I suggest you take the cabs and use the car only when absolutely essential."

Flint glimpsed around the apartment once more. Then his eyes came to rest on the double bed in the far room. It was suddenly apparent to him that he was quite tired from the long flight from California. In his younger days it wouldn't have meant a thing. But he was feeling the strain of the travel now.

"Look, Georgio," he said, "I'm a bit bushed. Let's finish unpacking my stuff and then we can go over some of the details on this whole mess. I assume Harry has some procedure he wants carried out. At least those finer points we didn't get to discuss on the phone." He brushed a lock of hair from his forehead and resumed unpacking his bags.

"By the way," Flint added, "what is the other option of travel?"

"Oh. You can walk." Georgio answered without hesitation. "Saratoga isn't all that large. Except you might be moving to some of the smaller, surrounding towns during your investigation. That will require a car. This is still considered rural territory by most people. They don't have buses, either."

"Harry didn't mention anything other than Saratoga," said Flint. "But, then again, it's always what Harry doesn't tell me that . . ." he paused. "Oh. never mind. I should have figured there'd be some divergence. It's Harry's way, isn't it?"

"Another thing," Georgio insisted. "If you stay here most of the time, your coming and going should be by night. They do have snow removal on the front walks and the carriage road that divides the mansions in the rear. Most of this is done during daylight hours, though. Other than that, I can't think of any other precautions." His eyes lifted to Flint's. "I don't know why I'm giving you all this fatherly advice. You know more about this type of thing than most. Anyway, Harry is very concerned about what's happened here. We don't want any repeats."

When they had finished putting everything away, Georgio pulled out a map of the area and began circling parts of it with his pen. After a minute or two, he stopped, held up the map and gave a long sigh.

"Somewhere in this region there's a figure moving about that knows the answer to Robin's murder. Who he is. What he is. That's for you to find out."

"You said he," Flint interjected.

"I guess I did," Georgio said.

Flint pointed a finger at the ceiling. "Maybe the he is a she. Maybe both. We never assume otherwise until we know. Do we?"

A good cop keeps an open mind," Georgio agreed.

Laying the map on the counter, Georgio proceeded to outline the area, town by town, village by village. Some of the names Flint knew by memory. Others he hadn't ever heard of, nor faintly recognized. The changes in the past 20 plus years were apparently enormous.

Now, tracing his finger over the roads, including the interstate highway, he realized that the Saratoga he knew in the '60s and '70s was indeed a very different place. It would take some time to acclimate himself to all the changes.

Georgio leaned forward and began pointing at spots on the map away from Saratoga proper.

"This is Schuylerville," he said, the pinky finger trailing to a hamlet near a river to the east. "We're pretty sure they transport dope through here in the summer months. It's easy, because they can boat down from Canada on the Hudson River and tie up at a dozen or more marinas along the way. There's another public docking site at Mechanicville, a bit further south, also."

"Business must pick up in August," said Flint.

"Exactly," Georgio agreed. "They hold special rock concerts at the *Saratoga Performing Arts Center* over in the park, and on some nights, they pack in 35,000 or more. We've had reports that $50,000 worth of action can take place in a single evening during one of the shows." He bobbed his head to one side as if shaking water from his ear, and smiled again. "Not bad action."

Flint stretched his tired back muscles. "Robin reported on this?" he asked.

"She touched on it. But we have had reports from other sources for some time now," Georgio said.

"Proceed," Flint insisted.

"We've got Glens Falls to the north. It wasn't a problem, but since they built the Civic Center there a few years back, the same situation with the rock scene takes place. It's a shifting market. The peddlers follow the concerts. Most of the bands have their own people in on the action, too. We estimate they make as much off the dope as on door receipts on a given night."

"It's a cake walk. There's money and market up here," Flint said.

"It was a cake walk for someone," Georgio agreed. "But the cake is now being cut too many ways and that's causing some problems. Harry thinks New York and Montreal have been fighting over this territory, but neither wants an all out war for fear of drawing attention of the Feds to their very lucrative baby."

It was apparent to Georgio that Flint was getting very tired. His eyes blinked open and shut as they talked.

"Just a few more," Georgio said. "Over here to the west we have Ballston Spa. Not much action going down here. We then dip into Clifton Park to the south. Schenectady and Albany are the major cities to the south, but this is a mixed bag. Schenectady doesn't appear to be too bad. Small dealings. Not much money there to buy heavy. They've got a big freelance prostitution problem.

It's mostly local action. Lots of kids swinging on their own in the black community. Lots of clap being passed around, so the johns with money don't frequent the section often. Mostly local action. Ten and fifteen dollar stuff." He saw that Flint was fading fast. "Let's finish this all in the morning," Georgio sighed. "I'll give you everything we have to date. It's yours from there, OK?"

He looked down but Flint didn't answer. He was already asleep in the chair.

4. The Double-Take

F lint sat in the small kitchen sipping coffee and reflecting on the information he and Georgio had gone over. Georgio was on his way back to New York, and the task at hand was to filter through all the facts and hearsay, sort out what might be important and relative to his investigation, and try and implement a course of action.

The problem was where, within the small but complicated boundary line of Saratoga, would he begin. He spent all day going over the data. It was now night and he hadn't ventured from the mansion. He decided to go for a walk, feeling safe that it was late enough and the area would be deserted.

It was still very cold out, so he dressed for the weather, wearing a dark pullover wool cap, three-quarter-length lined worsted jacket and grip-rubber-soled boots. He also wore woolen gloves. Once down the stairs, he quickly moved through the large main room to the side doors. Hesitating for just a moment before going out, he adjusted his collar up over his neck.

He then stepped out into the bitter, windswept night. He stayed close to the building, walking toward the rear where the wide road separated the mansions. He could hear and feel the icy snow underneath, crunching on the soles of his boots. He turned right and walked slowly in the direction of the far street where Georgio had said the all-night gas station was located.

On either side of him, the silent, deserted mansions, one after the other, stood dark and lifeless. He could hear the wind striking against their oversized windows and whistling about and through the dozens of chimneys. Huge bulks of granite and stone that had served the rich and famous so well for years were now orphans of another time.

It took him about seven minutes to reach the end of mansion row. He walked a bit further, reaching the street. He could make out the dim light of the gas station some 100 yards to his left. But he was not about to go in that direction on this first venture out. Instead, he turned right and walked past the last mansion and again turned right heading back toward his own nest. There was nothing but darkness about him. Darkness and the noise of the night wind. A double-width road was on his left, and across the road were woods. He walked in continuing silence. It reminded him very much of a time when he had walked Russia's Red Square in winter. Bleak, with unforgiving cold.

As always he kept a keen alertness to everything about him. About halfway home, his eyes were drawn to a great, pillared portico of the second to last mansion before his.

Suddenly he realized that he had seen the structure before. He paused at the entrance to the long driveway, looked again, and then decided to have a closer look. He moved slowly up the driveway and came to a stop just short of the portico. Could this be, he whispered to himself? Yes, it must be. He went to the porch and approached the large twin oak doors. It was very dark under the portico. He reached in and took a small pen-sized flashlight from his pocket. Covering it with one hand, he flashed it for a moment on the metal plaque on the front door. The initials HH appeared.

So here he was, in the middle of winter, standing on the porch of the very home in which he'd known so many wonderful times; had once danced in its large inner main living room to string orchestra music and walked in and about its summer gardens with its kidney-shaped swimming pool and its ornamental statuettes adorning the garden walls. All the warm, exciting people that had come to the Holmes residence in those days, suddenly started flashing across his memory.

Unconsciously, he began walking toward the rear of the mansion, stepping slowly on the driveway's soft snow where the wind had piled it up in small foot-tall heaps and drifted it up to the sidewalls, just short of the lower windows.

Here on this bitter winter night, he could feel and sense the presence of them all. And, on the night's wind, he could almost hear their voices. For a moment he felt a great wanting for that time and an inner loneliness.

He waited, staring out at the deserted garden full of snow and the more he stared, his imagination wandered on to one particular evening in the garden when the then Vice President of the United States made an appearance to help celebrate Harrison Holmes's birthday.

He was then aware that he was getting colder standing there. His body began trembling slightly. His blood, still California thin, was far from having acclimated to Saratoga's severe deep freeze.

Flint wondered, not for the first time in his line of work, where this investigation would lead.

Who would be the culprit? Or would there be many culprits? As always, everything was a big, unsolved puzzle. Piece by piece, he would have to fit the parts together. And he knew it could not be a hurried thing. It would be very difficult doing it alone, he reasoned silently to himself.

As uncomfortably cold as it was, Flint didn't want to return to his apartment just yet. So he continued walking toward downtown Saratoga. Partly out of curiosity and partly to see just how long a walk it would be. He eventually came out at Circular Street, just opposite historic Congress Park. He walked past the park to Broadway. The snow by now was four inches deep and, as if he were a kid again, he kicked it forward with his boots with each step.

It was almost 8 p.m. and Broadway was quiet of motor and pedestrian traffic, though there were lights in many of the shops. He immediately recognized this main section of town. He moved along the right side, past an open lot where the Quinn family once had their popular *Colonial Restaurant* until fire destroyed it in the early 1970's. On the opposite side of Broadway he stopped to peer at the *Rip Van Dam Hotel*, still active since the 1800s, and the restored *Adelphi*, two sentries of Saratoga's golden years. He was chilled enough now so that he felt he needed a stiff drink. Brushing snow from his shoulders, he pushed through the highly glazed, wooden doorway of *Lillian's* restaurant, a place he neither knew nor ever heard of, save for the name that had a familiar ring to it.

Once past the foyer and into the bar area, he suddenly realized why the name had meaning. There were two large black and white framed photos hanging on the back bar. One of Lillian Russell, the other of "Diamond" Jim Brady. It amused Flint to think that after all these years, the two early stellar visitors to Saratoga were, in a manner of speaking, still imposing their personalities on the little town. Legends die hard, he mused.

Lillian's was crowded. He elbowed his way to the far end of the bar and, catching the bartender's attention, ordered a double brandy on the rocks.

He felt the drink's immediate sting revive his senses. He was also quite hungry. Every table was filled, but he put his name on the waiting list anyway. He was about to order another brandy when a tall, cute, red-headed hostess tapped him on the shoulder. "If you don't mind sharing a table, I can seat you now," she said.

"I'm not choosey," Flint replied, as the hostess lead him to a table near the front window section where two girls were already seated.

"I hope I'm not intruding," he said, not seating himself until he was assured of his welcome.

"Of course not," said one girl looking up at him. She was a slender-faced, short haired blonde with a pleasant smile. She extended her right hand to Flint. "I'm Ellen Smith," Then, directing attention to her dining mate, added, "This is Sandy Blair."

Sandy lifted her head from the menu she had been reading and Flint, staring back into her dark brown eyes and exquisite facial features, nearly gasped. Though he knew it wasn't possible, he was beholding Alice's face. He stepped back and stared again. The perfectly structured jaw line, the long dark hair, the calm dark eyes.

Even in *Lillian's* all too uneven dining room light, Sandy, for all practical reasons, was Alice, except for her eyes. Though Sandy's eyes did not have the liveliness of Alice's, Flint, being a good judge of people's moods, sensed that Ellen and Sandy had been in a deep discussion before he came to their table. Talk apparently cut short upon his arrival.

"Yes. Well, that's great. I will join you," he said. Unable to take his eyes off her face. Once seated, he was looking straight at her, hoping that she did not detect any hint of surprise on his face.

"My name is Mike," he said, purposely avoiding dropping his last name.

"*Lillian's* is very popular," said Ellen. "It's generally packed here. We often share tables with diners."

They passed small conversation back and forth over a drink which Flint insisted on buying and he appreciated their company. All during dinner, though, they engaged in verbal pleasantries, there was little or no real probing of each other. Flint did, on several occasions, flash a glance at Sandy, for he was still bewildered and enthralled at the resemblance.

Then dinner was over and Ellen and Sandy, wishing him well, departed, while Flint nursed his last drink. He watched as they picked up their coats from the checkroom and left. He slouched casually in his chair thinking about what he'd just experienced. Maybe, he was thinking, too many years of being single, and age, were getting to him.

He made his way back to the apartment, noting that it had taken about 26 minutes.

5. Happy Birthday, Sweetie

Sandy Blair woke up early this cold, February morning to a rush of wind outside her third story apartment bedroom window which faced historic Congress Park and the even more historic *Canfield Casino.*

It was not yet 6 a.m., yet the first gray light of day streamed through the overly large window and came to rest on her twin-sized bed. She blinked open her eyes to check the clock once more before getting up.

She was due at the Saratoga Hospital at 7 a.m., sharp, but she felt very tired and really didn't want to get up from under the warmth of her down comforter this morning.

The sudden winter cold spell that had been gripping Saratoga for the past week, was made even more unpleasant by the snow that had suddenly come down out of Canada on the shifting jet-streams.

It was such a lovely, warm town in summer, she was thinking quietly, but from January through March, it could resemble Siberia at times. This was one of those times.

Ten minutes had slipped by since she was first conscious of the light of day, so with some effort she finally moved from the bed to the bathroom to take her daily shower.

When she was done, she dried off quickly, rubbed some body powder over her breasts, arms and legs, and then dried her long dark hair with the blow-dryer. She did this all within twenty minutes. As a registered nurse with a B.S. degree, she had become accustomed to early morning hours, and getting ready within a half hour, though it had taken some practice over the years, was something she was now used to.

She stood near the window, combing her hair. First full out to the sides, and then tighter on the sides. Finally pulling it tight on both sides and back, and securing it with several bobby pins.

When satisfied with her hair's appearance, she dressed in her freshly-pressed nurse's uniform and then fastened her gold RN pin to the collar.

She was as ready as she could be considering that her brain had not fully begun to function and her stomach was still a bit off from having eaten a late evening pizza at the all-night pizza place on Division Street, following a small house party for one of the doctors. One should never party in mid-week. Wasn't that what she had told herself many times over? "But we won't stay long," they would say. "We'll just drop in for a short while. Come along. You'll have fun."

Yet it really wasn't the party, nor the late-night pizza for that matter that had her tired. It was a dream she had during the night about being in some sort of boat accident up on Lake George, some forty miles north of Saratoga.

Why, she asked herself, would anyone dream of being in a boat on Lake George at this time of year. And why an accident? And a fatal one at that?

She had gone to bed about 1 a.m. but the fearful dream disrupted her sleep about 3 a.m. The balance of the time was spent twisting and turning, and waking to the intermittent recurrence of the dream.

Now, sitting at her small vanity, she stared at herself in the mirror for several moments. Slowly she put the finishing touches to her makeup, though she wasn't in the habit of using too much. Her mother had always cautioned against overly painting one's face and losing the natural beauty of one's youth.

"There will come a time in life," her mother's words still echoed in her ears, "when you will have no choice but to use cosmetics. Pretty young girls don't need it."

Well, she decided, I'm not that young little miss with the dark ringlets trailing below my neck. A touch of moisture liquid makeup, a slight brush of eyelash mascara and a soft blend of red lipstick, was needed. Not to be overdone, as Mother had preached, but to give a twenty-six-year-old face a morning lift. A fresh start on the day.

As she applied the last bit of lipstick, she was startled by her phone ringing loudly. She reached for the small, white designer receiver after the second ring.

"Sandy here," she said with her voice not yet in full pitch. "Happy birthday, sweetie," came a greeting she hadn't expected.

"My god," Sandy said, recognizing the female voice. "Someone remembered! And I'm glad because I had completely forgotten about it."

It was Helen Foster, one of Sandy's dearest friends from the hospital. "Don't think for a moment I'd let you forget your big day," laughed Helen. "Besides, it gives me a good excuse to take you out to dinner."

"You don't have to do that," Sandy said. "It really should be my treat."

"No," Helen insisted. "It will be my treat. And

we're going to do it up right. How about doing that new French place up in Corinth?"

"Not St. Sophie?"

"Why not" Helen said. "I'll pick you up about seven or so. You're off work at five, aren't you?"

Sandy knew from others that a meal for two at *St. Sophie's* was going to run over eighty bucks. In her estimation, Helen was being too generous on her offer.

"I'll settle for a good steak at *Sperry's*," she tried vainly to persuade Helen. "We can do *St. Sophie's* another time."

Helen, anticipating this, closed off the phone call with a short, "Oh, I can't switch now. My mind is set on French food, and I know you'll love it. See you at seven, sweetie. Have a happy..."

Sandy heard the phone click off at the other end.

She took one more look at herself in the mirror. Twenty-six or not, she mused to herself, I'm still quite beautiful. Aren't I?

Helen's phone call had been a pleasant surprise. It gave Sandy the spark she needed and, thinking about it, she was really happy that Helen had suggested it, because she had a curious craving about the place.

Sandy had been well schooled in the refinements of dining at fashionable restaurants around Boston, Washington and other places when she was living with her parents, but Saratoga in winter offered no real extravagant eating places. Already, in her mind, she tasted the tangy flavor of rich, French onion soup, followed by heaping mouthfuls of duck, washed down with a delicate wine, served in a hand engraved goblet. Yes, *St. Sophie's* was a fine suggestion.

One glance at her table clock quickly brought her out of her imagined dining experience. Hell, she thought, I'd better make it out of here in a hurry, or I'll be late for work.

She gave herself a dazzling birthday smile in the mirror, slipped on her dark blue winter coat, wrapped a scarf about her neck, put on fur-lined boots, remembering to carry her work shoes along in a bag, and headed out of her apartment.

The apartment house was located on the corners of Broadway and Phia Streets, and Sandy had the option of leaving the building on either street. This morning she chose Broadway, and as she came out the apartment's front entrance, a brisk, bitter wind hit her squarely in the face. It was the coldest day she could remember since the season had started.

She proceeded up Broadway, walking on the east side of Saratoga's main downtown shopping district, then crossing about midtown, near the old *Worden Hotel* which had been a favorite watering hole for famous actor Monty Wooley until his death. She continued along Broadway until she reached the corner of Church Street, where the hospital was located. As was her routine, she stopped in at the corner newsroom to buy a morning paper.

Three or four Saratoga regulars were huddled near the counter, talking to Salty Meade, the newsroom's owner. They all seemed engrossed in excited conversation. Sandy tried twice to pay for the paper, but her presence went unnoticed. Finally she just threw a quarter on the counter between them and started for the door. She had it half open when Salty called after her.

"Miss . . . Miss. Can I have a word with you?"

Sandy swung around. "What is it, Salty?"

He motioned with his hand for her to come to the counter, while at the same time shooing the others to one side.

He spoke in a soft, almost inaudible tone.

"Weren't you a close friend of the girl up on 10th Street?"

Sandy shook her head in a puzzled, yet acknowledging, yes. "I thought so," said Salty, his small round eyes squinting at her in a frightening stare.

Suddenly Sandy thought of Robin and her heart began to beat very fast. Then, after a moment of stillness, she found herself asking, "What about her? What's happened?"

"Hell," said Salty, "ain't you aware of all the stirrin' with the cops around this area this morning?"

"I've just come from my apartment," Sandy replied innocently. "I haven't seen anything."

Salty's normally reddish face, drained to a pale white, and his voice faltered. "She's been murdered. The poor girl has been murdered," he finally was able to say.

Sandy could feel her body beginning to shake all over. At the same time, a sudden inner rage and the urge to scream gripped her whole being, but she managed to suppress it.

"The cops have been everywhere," Salty continued. "Some have been in and out of here. One said that she had been drowned, but I don't understand what he means. It's a terrible thing."

Sandy went to the door and looked out through the glass. She could make out some police cars further up the block, but observed no unusual movement. And her mind began working intently. The vision of Robin as Sandy had last seen her alive, smiling at her from a street corner just a few days ago. Wishing each other well, and making a tentative date to meet for lunch or dinner, depending on Sandy's schedule at the hospital. Robin's silly, yet characteristic wool cap, tipped on the back of her head and wearing a jacket that Sandy knew wasn't the proper weight for the winter. Yet always smiling, always trying to look cheerful, even though her problems were many.

Tears swelled now in Sandy's eyes. Her hands couldn't wipe them away fast enough. She reached in her purse for a tissue, but Salty's trembling hand was already there, holding out a fresh handful of tissues. She took them and wiped away more tears while fighting to hold back the urge to scream again. She put the soft tissues to her face, and then over her mouth to hold back the involuntary moan that was coming from her throat.

"Robin," she said aloud, so that everyone in the newsroom looked at her. "Robin," she repeated. Then she went quickly out of the newsroom, still clutching the tissues and holding them to her face.

From the rear she heard Salty pleading with her to come back, but she started up the block toward Robin's apartment house, not thinking clearly nor caring of anything, her mind racing chaotically, the cold air crystallizing the tears on her cheeks, walking at a steady pace toward the building ahead.

From a distance of some one hundred yards, she could make out a group of people huddled outside the front entrance. But they were nothing more than a blur of bodies at this far point and she couldn't tell whether or not they were police. She picked up her pace, fighting the bitter wind and finding the walking a bit more slippery as she went along. In her mind she kept telling herself that she had to go to Robin's building, that she had to see and hear for herself that it was true. Yet she was scared and bewildered by this obsession to go there and see what had really happened.

One step after the other, she kept going, slow-ing her pace now as she got to within thirty yards of the building. Now she could make out the people in front. There were several men and women and, she noticed, three uniformed police. One was leaning on a squad car parked at the curb and the other two apparently guarding the entrance.

She simply walked right up to the front entrance, looked at the police guards with a placid, indifferent stare, and without even realizing her movement, entered the building. The guards said nothing, so she continued for a few more steps until she was well within the downstairs hallway. Then, suddenly coming to her senses, she was aware what she had done, and suppressed, inner fright quickly became instant panic. Cold beads of sweat rolled down her back. She was scared and shaking as she realized that she was standing within the same structure where Robin had died just hours earlier.

Then, on the second floor, there came voices. Low at first. Then louder. Sandy listened, but the voices were drowned out by heavy footsteps clicking along on hard wooden floors. She listened further. The footsteps stopped, then continued. Sandy's attention was then drawn to the long, wide staircase to the right of the hallway.

Two women were coming down the stairs. Both had on winter overcoats, hats and boots, and one was about a foot taller than the other. For some strange reason Sandy thought they were laughing. But as they drew closer, Sandy noticed that the shorter one was actually very upset and the taller one was trying to console her. Sandy was not exactly hidden from their view, but because of their apparent preoccupation, neither saw her.

As the two reached the main entrance, the shorter woman let out a cry that echoed throughout the old building. Outside, pausing to look back, she let out another cry, at which one of the policemen went to her assistance. She finally settled down and was led away by her friend.

During all of this time, Sandy had stood in the same place in the hallway. Then she over-heard one guard say to the other, "That woman was utterly hysterical."

"It's enough to make anyone hysterical," said the other.

"I guess you're right," said the first guard.

For what seemed an interminable time, Sandy remained standing in that spot. Eventually she just turned and walked back to the entrance and went outside. In the brighter daylight, her eyes seemed like glazed china. She had continued to form tears all the time she was in the building and the cold air gelled them to her eyelashes.

"You can come and go to your apartment, Miss," she was aware of someone talking to her, "but don't go inside the marked off perimeter on the third floor. It's off limits until further notice."

She spun about to face one of the officers smiling at her. So that was it, she thought, he thinks I live in the place.

"It's unpleasant, but we'll be done with our business soon," the officer further reassured her.

"Yes. Fine. Thank you," was all she could man-age to say, and at that she began walking back toward her apartment and not to work as she had originally planned. She could not work. She was completely unprepared for this tragedy and in addition to feeling almost overpowered by grief, she was beginning to feel faint and nauseated. Work would have to wait. She needed to go right home.

The only thing that kept her from passing out was the cold morning air sucked into her lungs. Actually it was below freezing at this point in the day, but the penetrating wind was not her enemy, nor was the snow or ice. Sandy's imagination was playing tricks on her as she hurried home and it descended into her very depth. She now began to conjure up all sorts of frightening thoughts.

The power of mere suggestion was taking over all logic and reasoning, adding to the general miseries of the morning. What really had happened to Robin, anyway? Sandy had managed to walk into the very building without even asking the police, or anyone else for that matter, what had happened. She had only Salty's words to go on, and she took them to heart without further questioning.

She quietly asked herself, "Was it because she had had the feeling right along that Robin was in great danger? That each time they met, Robin showed it in her face and eyes. Even came close once to mentioning it, but hesitated short of actually saying just how bad things were getting for her in Saratoga."

It was amazing how nervousness could alter one's body and mind, she was now thinking. How, under pressure, one could lose control of oneself. How the uncertainty of the situation, with all its dire implications, could take hold and distort reality.

I must pull myself together, she further thought. I must get home and sit down and work this out for myself. Then the thought also came to her to call her office and talk to her boss, Dr. Blake. Yes, she admitted quietly, he would be the one to talk to.

Sandy almost stumbled as she reached the curbstone at the corner of Broadway -- a car turning right honked its horn at her, its driver shaking his fist in anger.

She crossed Broadway and kept going. In the

sudden turn of events, she hadn't given any thought to her personal involvement with Robin, and had really never considered nor envisioned the danger Robin exposed herself to. Oh, Robin had talked about strange things. About doing some sort of secret work for some guy in New York City, but she never revealed the details. There were times when Sandy actually believed Robin was making it all up. That these stories were more of an attention getter.

"It was true. It was true," Sandy repeated wordlessly. And then she recognized that anyone who had befriended Robin could very well find themselves in jeopardy. Or was she merely letting her imagination run wild with unfounded, needless assumption?

She had to talk to Dr. Blake. He would know what to do, how to cope with the situation. After all, he had been Robin's assigned psychoanalyst for over a year. The deep, dark secrets that haunted Robin no doubt had been revealed to Dr. Blake.

She ducked into the hallway of the Adirondack Trust Bank on Broadway and went to the wall phone and immediately dialed Dr. Blake at his hospital office.

Through two large glass doors, she glanced at the bank clock on the far wall and noticed that it was now 7:32 a.m. It was probably too early for Dr. Blake to be in the office, but she let the phone ring anyway. To her surprise, he answered after the fourth ring.

With her voice still shaky, she identified herself to Dr. Blake, saying in quick succession, "Robin is dead. Robin is dead."

He replied in a much firmer, yet settled voice, "I was given the news about an hour ago. The police called me and said they had found my pen in the pocket of one of her coats. Like yourself, it took me by complete surprise. She was a sweet girl. A caring girl."

"I'm at a loss," Sandy said. "I can't come to work. I'm shaking all over. What shall I do, Doctor?"

There was a long pause on the line, then he finally answered her. I think it best that you go straight to your apartment. I wouldn't advise coming over here. The police will be back for further questioning, and I see no reason to get you involved in the middle of their investigation. Stay at the apartment at least for the next couple of days. I'll cover you with an excuse here at the hospital."

"I don't know if I can go it alone right now," she sobbed. "I'd like to come and talk."

"It isn't in your best interest," said Dr. Blake. "Do as I say for now. We can get together when things are worked out at this end. It's the best advice I can give you right now, Sandy. Please believe me."

"If you think it best," she agreed. "I'll do what you say, Doctor. I'll go right home."

"Sandy," he added, "make sure to lock your doors. And don't use the phone if you can help it. I'm not implying that you're in any immediate danger. I just think it best to play this thing low key until we can find out what really happened today. It's all very sordid at this point."

She could think of nothing more to say, except to add, "Will you promise to call me later tonight? I'll stay up till twelve or so. In fact, I doubt if I can sleep at all."

"Yes," he assured her. "I'll call later. Now get home and try to relax. Everything will be fine."

Sandy had long admired Dr. Blake's way of speaking with a slow, compelling authority, the way he talked to most of his patients. He could make you feel at ease with just a few words. After hanging up the receiver, she lingered for a few minutes, feeling better for having made the call. Then she resumed her walk home.

The sun was out and shining now, and it flickered and reflected off the many storefront windows, the same windows that so often she had stopped to browse in during the holiday season when they were brightly lit and full of the latest clothing, shoes and other apparel. She made no attempt to look one way or the other this day. Her focus was straight ahead, her mind and senses still numb from the day's proceedings. All she could see was Robin's smiling face.

The pure, simple honest expression of a girl who was reaching out for friendship and love, trying to make it in a town indifferent to her troubles. Together, Sandy remembered, they had walked this street both day and night on occasions. During the warm dog days in August when the racing people were in town, and on snowy evenings when Broadway was all but deserted. They knew every store by heart, but enjoyed going back each time. Robin had once remarked, "We're the window shopping twins."

Halfway home she passed in front of *Lillian's* Restaurant and, giving a quick glance at the two large, highly polished wooden entrance doors, her heart pained as she remembered the many happy times she had spent dining with Robin at *Lillian's*.

She found the walking a bit easier. Most of the store sidewalks had a fine layer of sand applied over the hard packed ice and snow, with a combination of sand and rock salt covering some of the walks.

She walked a little faster on the firmer footing, calming a bit now that she was but a short distance from her apartment building. The instinctive feeling of safety that one seems to realize when approaching home gave Sandy more confidence with each step.

Many Saratogians opted to hibernate in winter rather than fight the elements. Sandy, on the other hand, always enjoyed winter outings. Though the cold she felt now, she felt deep inside, and it was chilling to the bone. She was also cognizant that this chill was not fully attributed to the temperatures of the morning. It was more a chill of fright and uncertainty. She knew in her heart that Robin's death would somehow make everything unsettling from here on.

Thinking more about Robin, she felt a strange stir in her stomach. She had not felt this way since her father had died when she was but twelve years old.

She was so immersed in thought, she walked right past her building, stopping only when she raised her head and was aware that she had gone too far. In fact, she was almost to Congress Park, meaning she had crossed over Union Avenue, where there was a stoplight, without knowing it.

She waited for a moment, caught her breath, and then turned and went to her building entrance. She fumbled for her key in a pocketbook much too full of miscellaneous items. Once the door was open, she virtually flew up the three flights to her apartment, holding the door shut with her back once she was inside and then locking both the key lock and dead bolt.

Then she sat down and began to cry. Softly at first and then louder. It was the first real cry she had in quite some time and she did not even try to hold it back.

She let out all her emotions. Her hurt, her sadness for Robin and, in some respect, her self pity. She suppressed only the great inclination to scream aloud.

When she could cry no more, she finally went to bed, pulling the drapes of her bedroom window tight to block out the sunlight and burying her face deep into her down pillow.

She tried to force sleep, but it was no use. Her body was already rested. Instead, she lay very still thinking about Robin and restructuring in her mind the sometimes convoluted alliance they had shared.

Alone, remembering, Sandy knew this would be one of the longest days of her life. She needed someone to talk to, but there was no one she could think of to call. Dr. Blake said he would be in contact. She would have to wait for his call.

6. It's Your Pen, Doctor

T om Nealy has been Saratoga's police chief for twenty-five years. He strolled up the front walk to the Saratoga Hospital in his normal, slow-gaited style and entered through the large revolving glass doors.

Nealy was no stranger to this institution. During his years of service on the force, he had been in and out of the hospital on hundreds of occasions, tending to persons involved in shootings, rapes, muggings, auto accidents, snake bites, and any other kind of emergency a cop encounters in the course of his job. He had spent some personal time there, once having been admitted for a gallbladder operation. He had also been there on several social occasions, most recently attending the dedication to the new children's wing. Hospitals and cops have very much in common, he was thinking. They often see life's trimorphic side. Birth, sickness and death. It is routine duty.

Today's visit to the hospital was the first of a kind for Nealy and as he approached the receptionist's desk, he felt a bit uneasy about this particular call. It was the first time in his memory, that he had to call on one of the hospital's leading doctors about a homicide case that, in effect, could actually implicate the doctor being questioned. It was all very unsettling to Nealy.

His generally good-natured smile was not working this morning as he addressed the girl behind the desk. She stared up at Chief Nealy with small, rounded blue eyes that looked somewhat surprised to see the six-foot-three-inch uniformed head of police, standing with his arms on his hips, the brass on his visor gleaming under the overhead light. His eyes were serious, his mouth drawn tight.

"May I help you, officer?" she said.

His face seemed to relax some. He forced a smile. "Would Dr. Arnold Blake be on duty?" he asked in a soft, but firm voice.

"I believe he's here," she said. "I'll ring his secretary." While he waited for her to make contact, he observed the surroundings. The highly polished vinyl floors, the cream colored walls and the modern computers, three of them, set on a desk behind the receptionist. Red and blue drapes on the wide, tall windows, and what looked to be a new grid ceiling throughout the room and hallway. He also detected a faint antiseptic odor which, he surmised, was coming from the hospital rooms somewhere down the hall to his immediate left.

"Dr. Blake's regular secretary isn't in today," he heard the receptionist saying. "But the girl answering his calls says he is with a patient. He should be free in ten minutes or so."

Nealy handed her his official card, and again saw the surprised, wondering look in her blue eyes and the puzzled frown appear on her forehead.

"I'll wait," he said coolly. "Which way is his office?" She pointed toward the antiseptic flavored hallway.

"Down there," she said. "First right, then left

and it's your second door."

"Thank you Miss," he said tartly, his official voice betraying apparent apprehension at the interview he was about to conduct.

As he started for the hallway, she picked up the phone once again and called Blake's office. Nealy's instincts told him she would do this. No doubt the whole hospital would be buzzing about his visit within minutes.

Nealy was trying to think of an appropriate way to approach Blake. The right question, put in the right way, could mean all the difference in this ticklish situation. It was really a choice of confronting the good doctor with the facts at hand, or trying delicately to direct questions that would let the doctor voluntarily explain his relationship with Robin. He had never fenced verbally with a genuine shrink. There was a first for everything, he thought, but this particular encounter actually frightened Nealy some. He was right, nevertheless, about the strong odor coming from the hallway.

As he passed the first two or three doorways, he got another stiff blast of everyday hospital smell, sweet and somewhat sickening to his nostrils. He had never cared for hospitals under any circumstance, and the strong, clinical smell now was not at all pleasant.

He turned right at the far end of the hallway, as directed and continued a ways then turned left. Nealy hesitated a moment before entering the door that had Dr. Blake's name prominently displayed in large, black, raised lettering.

He read it carefully: *Dr. Arnold S. Blake, MD PC, Specialty -- Individual Psychotherapy For Adults.*

Then, in the right-hand pocket of his freshly pressed dark blue jacket, Nealy fingered a gold colored fountain pen. An object of much importance at the moment, because it had Dr. Arnold S. Blake's name and address inscribed on it. That fact in itself might not have been so startling except, and Nealy remembered being at the murder site at the time of its discovery, that it was found on the bathroom sink right next to Robin's hair brush.

The real, or imagined thought of Dr. Blake's involvement, sent a chill up the veteran police chief's back. If Dr. Blake were the murderer, it would be a revelation that could rock the tiny historical city off its foundation.

Nonetheless, Chief Nealy had to pursue the issue. He would not dare leave this phase of the investigation to anyone else in his department, though rightly it should have been conducted by detectives assigned to the city's homicide division. It was bad enough that Saratoga was faced with a major homicide. One involving a leading doctor, and a resident psychiatrist at that, would have to be handled with kid gloves. It would also be a public relations nightmare, Nealy reasoned. He didn't even want to contemplate explaining this one to the local, regional or statewide media. Not to mention the TV coverage and eventually, inevitably, the wire services leading to national inquiry and coverage. He had to spare his hometown this ultimate humiliation, if possible.

There was also a selfish side to Nealy's immediate concerns about publicity. Saratoga's police department had four other open murders on its hands, stemming over a five-year span. Of the five on-going investigations, only one was even close to being solved, and there were certain factions of the citizenry that complained that Nealy, now pushing fifty-seven, wasn't doing his job.

Besides, Saratoga, with its heavy dependency on tourist trade, and its prestigious Skidmore College on upper Broadway, had always been promoted by the Chamber of Commerce as being quaint, historical and safe, with the emphasis on safe.

The political fallout was another equation Nealy didn't want to think about. If he were to lose his job, a lot of old-time cronies would lose their positions also. And there was his retirement to consider. In three years' time, he could walk gracefully away from this thirty-seven thousand dollar chief's job and retire on about half his salary. Actually a bit more, if he took into account his four years in the Army during the Korean War.

His mind was spinning with a million and one "If's" as he finally entered Dr. Blake's office. For the first time in his career, he was really worried, more so than times when he had faced hard-bitten criminals with a gun in hand.

He went in and was met by a secretary. She directed him into an inner office, located at the end of a short corridor. It was dimly lighted. A desk lamp of very low intensity gave the room a faint, grey light. It picked up on the furniture, a wall painting and the blue and white drapes that covered a large window on the far rear wall. Dr. Blake was standing with his back to Nealy in front of the drapes.

As Nealy moved forward, Blake pulled the curtains apart, so that now daylight came streaming in. Through the window, Nealy could see the hospital's courtyard, with beautifully aligned white spruce trees and neatly trimmed hedges, covered with snow.

Blake seemed to be watching something for a moment, so Nealy just stood still and said nothing. Finally Blake turned and motioned Nealy to sit in one of the large upholstered chairs in front of an oversized mahogany desk set on top an overlapping area rug. It was an office that looked more like a study. It was a quirky collection of furniture, Nealy observed.

Blake sat down. Each man looked at the other. There was a dead silence, as if each was waiting for the other to break the ice. Nealy was about to speak, when Blake's voice cut through the quiet, his words coming slow and measured, as his deep-set eyes bore into Nealy's.

"It's about the murder, is it not?" Blake asked, taking Nealy by surprise.

Nealy's head jerked up. "I was on my way to the office and thought I'd cover a few things with you. The -- the investigation had led us to--"

"Please," Blake interrupted. "I knew you'd get around to seeing me. Or at least someone from your department. You can be as frank and as forward as you like in this matter."

Nealy was really taken off balance by Blake's admission. He had not expected this. He also didn't know how to interpret the remarks. On one hand, it appeared to be an outright confession. On the other hand, it could be a very carefully constructed statement, meant to disarm Nealy. After all, Nealy reasoned, this man is a psychiatrist.

Nealy's strong fingers gripped the hidden pen harder as he contemplated his next response. When finally he did speak, it came out in more of a muttered voice and, for a seasoned police professional, artless at best.

"I investigate all possible leads," he said. "I'm not certain of your involvement. Only you can tell me that."

Blake leaned far back in his black leather swivel chair, his eyes still fixed on Nealy's eyes, a forced smile on his pursed lips. Then he spoke again. "Do you come here with insinuations or facts, Chief?"

He verbally disarmed Nealy a second time, and

Nealy suddenly felt a knot in his gut.

Nealy then drew the pen from his pocket and set it on the desk. He waited for Blake's reaction, but there was none, at least no detectable reaction. Blake looked at the pen, then back at Nealy and asked quietly, "Does that pen represent anything of significance?"

Nealy touched the pen with his right index finger and, for the first time in the conversation, a smile of pleasure appeared at the corners of his mouth. *"IT'S YOUR PEN, DOCTOR. Perhaps you can tell me about it."*

Blake picked it up and studied it for a moment. Nealy, observing his composure, leaned back in his chair.

"Did someone give you this?" Blake inquired.

"Precisely," said Nealy, with his official tone of voice coming forth once more.

"May I ask who?"

Nealy rubbed his hands together and set them in a folded manner on Blake's desk. "I think you know where I acquired it," he said, again waiting to see any sign of surprise or disturbance in Blake's eyes.

"It could have been any number of people," Blake replied simply. "I've been handing them out to my patients for over a year now."

The knot in Nealy's stomach suddenly loosened and he sat up straight, the stiff collar of his uniform biting into his neck.

"That's an expensive pen, Doctor. You give them away?"

Blake opened a cabinet behind his chair and lifted out a small, red-colored carton and set it before Nealy. "Take a look for yourself, Chief."

Nealy hesitated. But Blake insisted. So Nealy opened the carton. A dozen or so identical gold pens were inside it. Nealy lifted one out and made a comparison.

"I'm running low on them," Blake said. "I'll have to place an order soon. They take six weeks or more to make them up."

Nealy was both relieved and embarrassed. "I suddenly feel very lousy, Doctor," he said. "But don't bother to understand. It's the nature of this work."

"It's not just cops that feel that way about their work," Blake added. "I cover all spectrums in my work. Yours is not unique, I can assure you."

Nealy finally began to relax. "I'm glad I was the one making the call this morning and not the team from homicide," he said. "They're probably better at this type of interview. They've got more scientific training in it, that's for certain. But I've got the whole community to think about. I hope you can understand my position."

"No matter what," Blake said, "your visit didn't exactly go unnoticed. No doubt the director will pay me a visit shortly to see what this is all about. There could have been a more tactful approach. I could have met you in town."

Nealy said nothing, instead he continued to stare at Blake with an embarrassed flush on his face.

Then it was Doctor Blake suddenly asking the question, "Where did you find the pen?"

Nealy showed some astonishment at this abrupt change in the conversation, though realizing at the moment that Doctor Blake was justified in asking it.

"It was found in the bathroom at Robin's apartment," he replied in a relaxed voice. Then just as stiffly added, "It stuck out like a sore thumb. It was laying on the sink, of all places."

Blake shrugged as if it hardly mattered. "I'm amazed," he said flatly. "Amazed that you'd assume what I feel you have assumed, based on finding one little item. Certainly all foreign objects discovered at a murder site should be taken into account. I can understand that, but I must say frankly that you got carried away on this one." He stared at Nealy. "Would you agree, Chief?"

Nealy sighed deeply. "Yes. I suppose you're right Doctor. Perhaps we've been under too much pressure lately. Maybe we've been going off half cocked. I don't have all the answers. I know the town is upset with our investigations of late, or what many in Saratoga believe is no solid investigation at all. But then, they sit on the sidelines. We get the duty to clean up this dirty mess as best we can. And we do with limited funds and resources. They want action, but they don't want to give me the proper manpower nor money to do the job right."

Blake grinned at him. "It's like all endeavors, Chief. You're supposed to do your job with humility. I understand what it's like to work without the proper resources. I face it every day here at the hospital. We do the best we can."

Nealy had picked up the pen once again and was tapping it lightly on the desk.

"Each patient receives a pen," Blake insisted. "It's just a way of reminding them to come back. Robin was a patient, but you probably already know that fact."

Nealy rubbed his chin with one long-fingered hand. "I never checked this point," he admitted, somewhat hesitantly, "though it should have been routine."

"Yes," continued Blake, "she was coming here for about a year. We admit some patients through the Social Welfare Department, but her situation was different. She came on her own one day. We provide mental health care service for those who can't afford it on a limited basis. She was one of those persons."

"Tell me, Doctor," Nealy asked with a pure

sense of curiosity, "was she a prostitute?"

Blake gazed up at the ceiling, pondering the question. "I would give you a direct answer if I could," he said, "but I don't reveal information on patients. We have confidential relationships, as most psychiatrist-patients do. If it were to come to a court order I might have to produce my files. But that's really up to you. I will say, on Robin's behalf, and knowing that you will keep it between we two, that she was not a prostitute, had never been a prostitute. In fact, she showed no signs of ever having experienced any type of casual or professional promiscuity. Besides this comment, I don't want to say anymore about her clinical involvement here. I hope you can appreciate where I'm coming from on this?"

Nealy stood up, his height now just being realized by Blake who was about a foot shorter.

"I think we've discussed this thing enough for one day," he said, drawing a deep breath and seemingly anxious to depart Blake's office.
"I'll be back in touch. I don't know exactly when. I certainly won't make a nuisance of myself. However, if I think it necessary, I'll call."

"Anytime," said Blake, meaning it.

Halfway down the corridor Nealy turned around and called, "What's really got us puzzled, is that we don't know what she did for a living. Might you know that?"

"I can't tell you because I don't know myself," Blake answered.

"This is a strange one," Nealy was heard muttering to himself as he disappeared down the hallway.

When Blake was certain he was gone, he quickly dialed Sandy at her apartment.

"Chief Nealy of the Saratoga Police has just left my office," Blake told her. "He was making inquiries concerning Robin. They found one of my pens in her apartment building."

He heard Sandy breathe heavily over the phone. "Doctor," she said with a quivering voice, "it must have been the pen I gave her last week when we went to dinner. I don't know if I can get through this terrible thing by myself. I'm scared all through."

"You must remain calm," Blake insisted. "It's hard on all of us. Stay where you are. Chief Nealy thinks Robin got the pen from me. He doesn't know of your friendship. I see no reason to bring this out in the open at this time. It can only lead to a lot of public and media scrutiny. Until I can find out further what really happened to Robin, I don't want the police or anyone else bothering you. Let me handle it from here. I'll call you tomorrow."

When he hung up the phone, he looked up and saw his Director, Ronald Stone, leaning in the doorway. He knew he was in for another several minutes of questioning. It was going to be one of those days, and he hadn't even seen any patients yet.

7. Talking With Horses

F lint was in a rage. He was now into his seventh week of the investigation, nothing was developing, the weather remained cold, he'd called Harry Waite four times and couldn't reach him, and Harry, for reasons Flint could understand, hadn't bothered to return his calls. Flint had stayed in his secret apartment all day and half the night waiting for Harry to make contact. By eleven o'clock, he figured Harry wasn't going to call, so he slipped on a wool sweater, a pair of warm gloves and a hat, and decided to go downtown for a few late drinks.

He was halfway down the stairs when the phone rang. He ran back and picked up the receiver.

"H.W.," a voice said.

Flint held the receiver for a time without speaking.

"This is H.W.," the voice said, deeper.

Flint said nothing.

"Come on, Flint, I know you're there. Say something."

"Screw you, Harry."

"Don't be like that, Flint. I couldn't call you earlier. I was busy."

"Look," said Flint angrily, "I don't put in social calls. When I call, it's for a reason. When you don't call back, I get to thinking...."

"Thinking what?" asked Harry.

"Thinking maybe I should have stayed in sunny California."

Harry's voice lowered. "Bear with me on this one," he said. "I just couldn't call you."

"All right," Flint agreed. "Let's change the subject. I understand there's a Canadian connection."

"What was that?"

"A Canadian connection," Flint said it slowly.

There was a prolonged silence on the phone. "Well," admitted Harry, "finally you've found out about Claude Morin."

"Let's say a friendly contact told me about Morin," replied Flint. "My contact says Morin has been doing leg work for you in both Montreal and Quebec."

"That's correct, Mike. We retained him on some small matter, if I recall correctly." Harry tried his best to pass this off lightly, but he could tell Flint wasn't buying it.

"Whatever," said Flint. "I understand he's your main contact in Canada, if not your only one."

"That's only natural," Harry injected. "After all, he's two-thirds French."

"No, Harry, he's all French-Canadian." Flint was having some fun with this exchange and he continued to stretch the point until finally Harry told him to go to hell about Claude Morin.

Harry changed the subject. "What have you got on the girl?"

"Nothing significant. In fact, there's nothing significant about Saratoga in the winter. You should know that, Harry."

"You've been digging around weeks now, Mike. Someone must know something?"

"I've got all the facts, Harry. I know all the joints she hung out in, her daily and nightly habits. I even have tabs on some of her acquaintances. But you know something, my friend? I don't think there's a soul in this town who knows who killed your Robin, nor cares about it."

"That tells me nothing," said Harry.

"On the contrary, it tells me quite a bit," Flint insisted.

"How do you figure?"

"I hope you're sitting down," said Flint. "I wouldn't want you to crash into your desk or something."

Harry's breathing quickened. "Get on with it, Mike. This conversation is getting far out."

"Her husband didn't do it," Flint said flatly. Then he waited for Harry's reaction. Again a long pause. Flint had time to take out a cigarette, light it and take three long drags before Harry responded.

"You've just ruined my entire evening unless, of course, you're deliberately trying to pull my chain," said Harry.

"Not on this one, Harry."

"Then my evening is shot."

Flint became more serious. "I'm not going into all the details now, but I found out that Robin's "ex" was dead for a week prior to her murder. So unless he came back as a ghost and scared her to death, we're now looking for someone else."

"Sweet bastards," yelled Harry. "This could be devastating to Central."

Flint continued. "I don't mean to ring your chimes, Harry, but you had better believe that someone up here knows about your operation. To what extent is what we have to figure out, and figure it out in a hurry. I also have another bit of local scuttlebutt. Perhaps you know about it, perhaps you don't. Anyway, the Feds are in town and have been since the track closed last August. I hear they're into this whole drug thing."

"Now you're destroying my whole week," Harry replied. "And for your information, I didn't know it was that heavy. Nor that the Feds were involved."

Flint laughed good-naturedly. "Relax, Harry. They're not chasing our fish. The Feds are interested in drugs of a different nature."

Harry flared. "I didn't know there was any other kind."

"Well, aside from the ones some jockeys are taking, there's a whole array of drugs for the thoroughbreds, and wouldn't you know, it's just as dirty a business as the street action you're familiar with."

"Who's feeding you all this?" Harry asked.

"I talk directly to the horses," replied Flint.

"Maybe the ones you're talking to are all doped up."

"No. I only talk to the straight ones. You should know that."

"Enough of this rot," said Harry. "I've got other things to do."

"So have I," said Flint. "Now that I have you on the phone, I want to speak my piece."

"Go ahead...say what you must," Harry said with a sigh.

"They're into new drugs that make horses run like hell. My sources tell me it will all come to a head sometime next summer or early fall. Hell, it could break right in the middle of next season's August meet. Anyway, there's lots of big names, including riders, trainers and owners...I understand the Feds have enough to put dozens away as race fixers."

"Jesus," Harry blared. "Isn't anything sacred these days? We've always known about the harness crowd shafting the system. Now you're telling me that thoroughbred racing is scraping the gutter."

"Dream on, Harry. Where there's money, there's mob. Have you ever seen it work differently? Though I must admit one would expect the New York Racing people to have better security... better control."

"Which families are involved?"

"My source didn't say. Both New York and New Jersey mob operatives have been identified, but there could be others."

Then Harry's tone changed again. "For a guy who can't find out much about my dead pigeon, you're certainly up on a lot of other things...why is that?"

"Abracadabra, Harry," he replied.

"What the hell does that mean?"

"Why, I thought an old scoundrel like yourself would understand that!"

"Let's say I'm dumb."

"It's the old hat trick, Harry. All magicians say abracadabra and everything comes out right. Except in this case nothing is coming out right."

"What are you driving at?"

"You've strung me far enough, Harry. And unless you fill me in on exactly why you dragged me to Saratoga, I'm jumping back into the hat and disappearing, just like that." He snapped his fingers.

Harry jumped on the defensive. "Perhaps you're assuming a lot of things that aren't so, Mike...Did you ever consider that?"

"Cut it right there, Harry. If you don't want to level, say so. But don't string me...I'm not stringable."

"I never thought you were. I didn't think it necessary to load all the barrels for you. If, however, you insist on knowing everything, I'll honor your request."

"Look," insisted Flint, "I know Central's operation as well as you do. Those masterminds in the backroom have a fetish for piecing out information...Keep 'em somewhere in the dark.. Caution against anyone knowing too much about any one facet of any operation...Walk slow...Milk 'em for all they're worth. It's all b.s. in my book, Harry. I'm on the line up here. If I don't know all the players I might come out the joker in this hand...I hope you're getting the message?"

"You're coming through clear. All right, Mike. I'll give it to you fast. We've known even before Robin's murder that someone was on to us. But it's been puzzling because it hasn't involved either local, state or federal agencies. Hell, if they wanted us out of Saratoga, we'd be long gone. The girl never figured to be a target. Shit. She didn't know anything of importance. That's why I figured her husband might have done it. Still, we couldn't take any chances."

Flint sensed that Harry was uncomfortable. His words came over the phone in long labored sentences.

"Listen, Harry," Flint quickly interrupted, "I know what you're going to say, but you can save it. My source already filled me in on just about everything that's been taking place up here. So save yourself a costly telephone bill. I also know that a lot of the action and problems are coming from Canada."

"If your source has been taking his lead from Morin, forget it," snapped Harry. "He'd sell his mother down the river if the price was right."

"You lose some, you win some," replied Flint. "I guess I have to go with my instincts and play my hunches."

"Remember, I didn't purposely mislead you, Mike."

"No. I never said you did, Harry. It's what you didn't say that's got me ticked off. For example, you never mentioned Franck St. Jacques either."

He could hear Harry draw in a deep breath, then his astonished reply.

"Where did that name pop up? Oh, yes, don't tell me...your source again!"

"Everything is coming home to roost," said Flint. "What the hell did you expect I would be doing with my time up here, talking to the birds? I get information. I'm good at getting information. That's what I'm paid to do."

"Look here, Mike, your source probably has told you that Morin's carrying a grudge because he feels he wasn't paid enough on his last assignment. Mark my words, he'll build a nest a foot thick in your ears if you let him."

"My source says St. Jacques is the Don of Quebec. Maybe Morin is playing both ends from the middle," Flint added. "I wouldn't trust him at all. But you know something, Harry, I've got just enough information to make me believe that Central is caught in a big squeeze...I'd go one further and say you've got something nearly equal to war between the New York and Canadian mobs. I haven't determined at this point whether they're positioning for dope, race fixing, diamonds, or perhaps all three. But it's very heavy stuff, and it may all be getting ready to blow in little ol' Saratoga this summer. I also think the only way I'm going to find out what really gives here is to visit Mr. St. Jacques' home base in Quebec City."

"That's not advisable, Mike. Those Canucks will eat you up and spit you out if they catch you across the border, and no one will give a damn."

"Why, Harry, I think you're trying to take the excitement out of my livelihood. Besides, I see no other way of piecing this whole mess together unless I do go up there."

"I can't support you on this," Harry insisted. "We haven't any solid contacts in Canada. It's the reason we involved Morin in the first place.

But, as I say, don't trust him."

"I'll brush up on my French," Flint laughed.
"Of course, the Canadians garble their French."

Harry said, "It's too risky. I'm begging you not
to go."

"I'm going anyway, friend. Wish me luck."

After he hung up the phone, Flint reached for
a cigarette. It was too late to go out now, so he
decided to retire. He went over some notes he
had taken earlier in the day -- mostly about
Robin's contacts and haunts in Saratoga. He
noticed she had made some visits to the mental
health unit at the hospital, though he didn't have
exact information on the nature of her visits. He
decided it was worth checking out.

He then pondered the Canadian situation.
February was nearly spent and the bitter cold
weather was giving way to warmer but windier
days and nights.

He suddenly realized how much he missed
his cottage in Palos Verdes Estates, and he fell
asleep dreaming of the warm Pacific Ocean waves
rhythmically tumbling onto the white sandy
beach outside his bedroom window.

8. Would You Care To Stay?

The next day Flint called Claude Morin and made arrangements to go to Quebec City. It had been a dozen years since he was last in Quebec, yet the memory of the old city was very clear in his mind. There was always the chance someone might recognize him, so he decided to slip in under disguise.

The chain of events over the past few days, including the mobs' apparent involvement, meant the assignment had taken on several new wrinkles. For instance, he wasn't quite certain he could conduct an effective investigation because of his restricted position once in Quebec. It ought not be too difficult getting around up there, but he would have to tread carefully on St. Jacques' turf.

He knew full well the tremendous risk he faced in crossing over to the Canadian side. A seasoned mobster like St. Jacques was no one to fool with and the Canadian gang was known for its ruthlessness. Flint considered them the worst of the lot, except maybe for the gangs that controlled the docks around Nice, or perhaps the mob men in Milan.

There was his decision on where to stay in Quebec, too. Morin, speaking in broken English, suggested Flint stay with one of his close relatives who lived in the center city. Flint politely turned down the offer. He wanted to be centrally located, but he also wanted to remain inconspicuous and as flexible as possible. He planned on getting in and getting out just as soon as he collected what information was necessary. He hoped his stay would not last more than three days.

If the Canadian mob faction were putting a move on the New York City boys in Saratoga, he intended to find out exactly what they were after. He couldn't understand why it was happening in a town of Saratoga's size. Logic said it didn't fit into organized crime's modern designs...but then, few people, including mob bosses, ever knew why certain moves were made, except it always centered on money He also wanted to go where there were crowds. He could always lose himself in a crowd if the occasion called for it.

He chose the grand old Le Chateau de Frontenac. He had stayed there many years earlier under different and more pleasant circumstances. Still he could recall its weatherbeaten stone facade, sinks as large as bathtubs, faucets that dripped, dimly lit long hallways, and its commanding location high on the cliffs looking down over the quaint old city. A very miserable and dreary place in winter, he also recalled, but very busy...an ideal place to stay to fit his purpose.

If, as Harry warned, Morin was not to be trusted, some evasive steps would have to be taken. Flint thought of a cover he had used once while on a mission to Spain.

It was an old trick taught him by an ex-Nazi spy who had employed it successfully in the early forties to avoid being caught by English intelligence while operating out of London.

The plan called for his registration at the Chateau under three separate names, taking a room on different floors and using a different disguise at each registration. He would not convey this cover to Central nor Morin. All contact during his Quebec visit would be by coded wire, and Morin, if needed, would be contacted only by phone. He would have Morin drop him off at the local bus terminal once they reached Quebec.

He packed a minimum of regular clothing because the disguises took up so much in his two luggage bags. He didn't take a hand gun...Morin would provide one after his arrival. While packing, a coded wire arrived from Harry. He slipped it into a slit in his belt, to be read later and digested. It no doubt was an update on St. Jacques' latest activities as best Central could put it together on such short notice.

His nerves were growing more sensitive to the trip ahead. He had felt this way before...too many times to remember. He contemplated it quietly, as he always did. The unanswerable question preyed on his mind. Would this trip be success-ful? By midday he was ready. He rented a car for the trip to Montreal where Morin would be wait-ing. Together they would drive in Morin's car to Quebec.

Before leaving Saratoga, Flint reviewed some notes he had scrawled on a scrap of paper a day earlier, noticing his last remarks about Robin's visits to Saratoga Hospital to see a Dr. Blake at the mental health unit. He checked his watch. He was not departing for Montreal until around 4:30 or so, which would give him ample time to make a call at the hospital to interview Dr. Blake. During his short stay in town, he had developed a maddening preoccupation over Robin's tragic death. His mind wouldn't let it rest. He now felt more strongly about finding her murderer than perhaps Harry Waite. He was also frustrated that he hadn't been able to get a lead. Not one solid lead. If he didn't unravel this one, it wouldn't be for lack of trying...he promised himself that much.

It came as no surprise to Flint that Robin probably found herself strangely alone in this small town, in spite of its homey atmosphere. He'd seen many people in the same position. He had seen them become unconscious of normal living patterns; deprived of life's better side, it was difficult to tell the natural from the unnatural day-to-day reason for existence. He pictured Robin as one of these people.

He drove to the hospital and went directly inside. The information clerk steered him to Dr. Blake's office, and a nurse on duty asked him to have a seat until the doctor was free.

Flint wanted to be as tactful as he could with this inquiry, certainly as careful as possible not to raise the least bit of suspicion. He carried a forged card which identified him as an insurance agent for American Life Insurance Co. of Toledo, Ohio. It was a nonexistent company, but the card appeared authentic and it had worked for him in the past.

"The doctor will see you now," the nurse said.

"Thank you," he replied, noticing as he walked past her that she was strikingly beautiful. He realized she must have felt his eyes on her neck, where the white uniform came in contact with her tanned shoulders. She blushed and he removed his gaze.

"Good day, Mr. Flint," the doctor greeted him, and he nodded.

"I take it from your card we have some insurance business to discuss?"

"Yes...yes."

"How can I be of assistance?"

Flint seated himself in a smooth leather chair at the doctor's motion. "I need some information on one of your, well, ex-patients."

"Who would that be?"

"Robin Smith."

Flint could see the doctor's nerves tighten under the skin, the small wiry black hairs on his forearms suddenly rise, and his eyes, a pale blue, take on a startled look. The reaction to his mention of Robin's name had triggered a response he hadn't expected. It was almost disarming him. He'd hit a vein with this medical man that bordered on shock.

It lasted but a second. Dr. Blake settled back in his desk chair and answered calmly, "She was a new patient here at Saratoga."

Flint stared straight ahead. "I know professional ethics won't allow you to reveal the exact medical help Robin was seeking, Dr. Blake. However, I'd like to try to piece together her movements during the last few hours of her life."

"Does it matter that much to the insurance company?" Dr. Blake asked.

"In this case it does."

"Strange," added Dr. Blake. "She came from rather meager surroundings. I'm surprised she even carried insurance...if, in fact, she did!"

Flint had to think fast. "It was an old policy. A thousand dollars face value. But it was hers." He hated to sit and tell lies like a trapped school kid, but it was necessary. He wasn't quite sure the doctor believed him.

Dr. Blake stood up and moved across the room to the window, his back to Flint. "Why not send the money to her next of kin?"

"We can't locate any," said Flint.

Blake turned around. "Who exactly are you, Mr. Flint?"

Flint's face showed no expression. "I'm an insurance agent, Doctor, just like it says on the card."

"I don't think you are," said Blake. "I think we

should end this discussion now."

Flint came out of his chair, uncoiling like a cobra from a basket. The talk was over, and he knew it, unless he could persuade Blake to continue.

He was madder than hell for having been too direct with his questions. There was an old adage in his line of work that said once an agent lost his ability to con someone, it was all downhill from there. He wasn't ready for the big slide, not just yet. He gave it another approach.

"As you say, Doctor, I'm not an insurance agent. Nevertheless, I came here because I want to help Robin...."

"It's a little late for that, wouldn't you say?"

"I'm tracking her killer...you've guessed that much?"

"I've guessed nothing, Mr. Flint. You could be her killer for all I know."

"I can prove I'm not," Flint snapped back. "But I'm not going to take the time to explain. You can believe me or not. If not, I'll leave."

Blake studied him for a time while slowly pacing up and down between the desk and the window. He stopped, smiled, and asked Flint to sit again.

"Did you call this office yesterday...say, three-thirty?" Blake asked.

"No," replied Flint. "Do you think I did?"

"Some man called. I thought it might have been you." Blake began rubbing his chin while leveling both eyes on Flint's face, as if waiting for him to admit that he did make the call.

"This is my first contact with your office," said Flint. "It had to be someone else."

"It was a weird call. At least I thought so."

"Why is that?"

"My nurse took the call."

"You said it was weird?"

"The caller wanted to know if my nurse knew Robin's address."

Flint turned toward the office door. "The nurse I met on the way in?"

"No," said Blake. "She wasn't on duty. It was Sandy Blair...she works three days a week for me."

Flint's memory mechanism flicked on...where had he recently heard that name mentioned? It started to come to him, then faded away.

"Do you know her?" asked Blake.

"I don't know. I've run into that name someplace...I know it was here in town."

"She lives nearby," said Blake, then adding, "Funny...that call came for me, but I have the feeling the caller was really trying to touch base with Sandy."

"I don't understand," said Flint.

"Well, when she told him I was busy, he kept her on the line and, as I said, he asked her if she knew Robin's address."

There was a sudden twinge in Flint's stomach. It wasn't a hunger pang...it was more like a sharp stab. "Your nurse...Sandy, could be in real danger. Where is she now?"

"It's her day off. She's probably at her apartment."

Flint jumped up. "What's her address?"

"My receptionist will give it to you."

"I'll go directly to her apartment," said Flint. "Let's hope the phone call wasn't what I think it was."

"What sort of danger is Sandy in?" asked Blake.

"That all depends," replied Flint.

"You'll have to be more explicit, Mr. Flint."

"If she knew Robin's address and said so to the caller, she might have been setting her up without knowing it."

He turned back halfway through the office

door. "Look, Doc. These people delight in murdering those who stand in their way, or who might have information harmful to their operations. Call your nurse and tell her to stay put, tell her who I am, and tell her to lock all doors until I get there...it's that serious."

Flint waited impatiently as Blake's lovely assistant scribbled down Sandy's address. He rushed out of the hospital to his car. He didn't even glance at her in his haste.

He moved behind the wheel, slipped the key into the ignition and accelerated out of the long driveway into late afternoon traffic. A gray sky had already begun to bring on evening and it looked as if it were about to begin snowing.

He spotted her building within minutes. He cursed under his breath at the parking situation near Congress Park. It was something he never quite got used to in Saratoga; there never was enough parking to go around.

Suddenly a car pulled out of a parking place near the opposite corner. Flint swung in a sharp turn, narrowly missing a jogger in the process, and pulled the nose of his rented Mustang into the space, bumping the curb hard with his right front tire.

His first observation was correct, the space wasn't big enough. He backed out, cut the wheel again and backed in. Yet it was still too small. He touched the gas pedal and his rear wheels squealed as the rear bumper locked with the car behind his, moving it back a foot or so.

"Now there's room," he said to himself.

He walked swiftly to the building entrance. He checked the names over the mail slots. Apt. 3-C. He pressed the bell. There was no answer. He waited a minute and rang again. A huge mahogany door with smoked glass windows and lace curtains guarded the entrance. He could make out a faint light in the inner hallway, but observed no movement. Beyond the light everything was dark.

After a time he stepped back into the street and looked up at the building. Only then did he hear the latch buzzer. The mahogany door swung open as he touched the brass knob and he went inside cautiously.

He looked for the stairs, but it was too dark at the other end of the hall to make any out. He eased his way toward the shadowy section, sliding his right hand along the wall as he went, hoping to find another light switch.

Pain...excruciating pain suddenly gripped his body. A blunt sensation in his stomach, more pain. Then he realized he had been hit with something sharp in the lower back, something that touched every nerve he possessed. Finally he dropped to his knees, though not unconscious. He detected movement to his left and, with what little waning strength he could muster, managed to avoid another blow, one that might have proved fatal in the grisly moment. A shiver ran down his body as a foot passed within inches of his head, and his assailant, missing the intended target, flew past Flint in the direction of the entrance door.

Flint had faced karate experts before, but had never received such a blow so unexpectedly. Had it landed nearer to the side, it might have broken all his ribs. Still he was thankful he was able to avoid the second strike. It gave him the precious few seconds to recapture his wits, to prepare his defense, to perhaps deliver a counter-blow.

He spun, still kneeling, facing his attacker. He couldn't see the face, however, nor really guess his size from his kneeling position, but he knew he was up against a seasoned fighter...a killer.

The stranger came at Flint again. This time slowly, hands waving in a circular motion, feet spread apart -- it was more a defense stance this time.

Flint was now on his feet, standing square to his attacker. Flint then moved slowly forward, crouching now, swaying his shoulders from side to side. His opponent made a sudden shift to the right which put him slightly off balance. Flint took advantage of this move and lashed out with his left hand, catching the stranger's right cheek just below the temple. He then drove his knee into the attacker's midsection. This forced the stranger against the solid mahogany door and Flint heard a faint moan as his opponent's body made contact with the hard surface.

Flint watched with amazement as the stranger slipped to the floor, out cold. He came forward and looked down, then poked at the body lying on its side, still and breathless.

He reached for a leg in an attempt to drag the body into the hall light. Suddenly the other leg shot around Flint's, tripping him in one swipe. Flint went over backwards, his head catching the corner of a hall table. Warm blood trickled down his face and soaked into his wool sweater.

He didn't have time to think about it, for the stranger came straight at him. Flint saw a knife blade flash in the light, and the thought of cold steel against his body sent instant fear through him.

He fell to one side, sticking a leg out to trip his opponent and striking a hard heel with the other. It found its mark and in one big thud, the attacker hit the floor, this time turning and twisting over. Though groggy, Flint jumped to his feet and braced himself for more battle.

There was a prolonged silence. Then Flint's ears pricked up as he heard heavy breathing. The breathing became more labored. It then turned to a gurgling.

Flint didn't make a move this time. He stood waiting, ready for anything. If his attacker was faking again, he would be in a position to react quickly.

The gurgling stopped. Except for Flint's breathing, the hallway was as quiet as a tomb.

Flint moved toward the body. He stopped within six steps of the heap on the floor. From that point Flint could see the knife handle protruding from his attacker's stomach. He appeared very dead, indeed.

A sudden flash of light appeared at the end of the hall. Flint turned around, his aching body springing to the defense once again, his eyes squinting at the glare.

"Oh, my God," he heard a female voice gasp.

"Down with the light," he ordered.

"What's happened?"

"Don't come over here," he said. "There's been an accident."

"Are...are you Flint?"

"I had better be," he replied, "or you're in trouble."

The girl holding the flashlight retreated a few steps.

"It's all right. I am Flint."

She moved closer. "I was frightened. I heard the noise, but I was scared to come down. I locked my doors like Dr. Blake said." Then, moving closer, she realized the man on the floor was dead.

"He almost got me," said Flint, a touch of anger in his voice.
"The bastard was tough!"

"What's this all about?" she asked.

Flint's head ached. Blood was still trickling down his face, though some had hardened on his hair, neck and clothing. "I'll tell you later, dear.

Right now we've got to get out of here."

She looked again at the dead man. "Don't you think we'd better call the police?"

"Not on your life," he replied, thinking as he said it what a silly reply it was under the circumstances.

"I don't understand!"

"There's nothing to understand. We're both alive this minute. That's enough understanding for me. Right now we're going to dump our friend in the cellar, if you have one, and we're splitting to safer ground. I can assure you there's more where he came from and they won't be far behind when they find out he's dead."

"Do you mean I have to leave the apartment?"

"I'm not trying to sound facetious, but from what you see here, would you care to stay?"

"I'll do as you say, Mr. Flint."

"I've got a place we can use for now. Gather up some of your clothing while I take care of our friend here. Make it fast."

The cellar stairs were old, narrow and winding, and Flint had a difficult time dragging the body to the basement. He deposited it in an unused coal bin.

He paused just long enough to take a look at his attacker's face and to make a quick search of his pockets. As expected, there were no papers nor identifying labels on his clothing.

Flint was well aware how close he had come to being killed in the fight. Then he noticed the boots. They were a special type, not often seen, with steel plates in the toes and heels, covered with leather of a shiny variety. It would have been certain death had one of those deadly weapons found its mark.

He studied the stranger's face. It was a sour face in death, and probably not much nicer in life. Flint couldn't determine the nationality. The nose was narrow and slightly hooked, the complexion dark, the eyes narrowly set, but his head was rather large for his height.

Flint suddenly had a thought. He took a piece of paper from his pocket, dabbed some moist dirt on the stranger's fingers and hastily took some fingerprints. He folded the paper neatly and slid it into his pocket, taking care so it wouldn't smear. If the killer's prints were on file, Harry would have them identified within 24 hours.

He then took an old, dusty blanket that was lying nearby and threw it over the corpse.

Once more upstairs, he found Sandy waiting in the hall. They went quickly out of the apartment building to his car and drove off toward Flint's place.

9. The Girl From Lillian's

Flint's head was really beginning to develop a slow, persistent pain, and the street lights blurred before his eyes as they sped along in his car.

Sandy sat tense next to him in the front seat. She said nothing. It had all happened too fast and her nerves were dancing throughout her body.

Flint cut a sharp right and turned down the street just below the mansion. He pulled to the curb and shut off the lights. Sandy started to open the door, but he cautioned her to wait a moment.

Then he spoke in a whisper. "When we get out, don't head for the mansion. Go up Bradford Street, the next one over. We'll get to the mansion through a back entrance."

"I don't understand," she said.

"I'm just playing it safe. Do as I say."

He then reached up and snapped out the car's overhead bulb, so that no light would show when they left.

"OK, let's move it," he ordered.

They walked silently yet briskly together on the dark street. He held her hand tightly, feeling the cold sweat on her palm.

Halfway down Bradford Street, he pulled her

to the right, almost causing her to lose her balance. He stepped a foot ahead of her, still gripping her hand, guiding her to a doorway. Without using the key or turning the knob, the door opened.

It was equally dark inside. It was a big house, she could tell, but she couldn't see anything. They went down a hallway, out through what appeared to be a kitchen or rear parlor, through another door to a courtyard. He directed her along a trellis-covered walk.

After fifty steps or so, they arrived at the back of the mansion. This time Flint reached down near the side of the back door and pushed a hidden button. The door slid open and they went inside. It closed tightly behind them. Flint then flicked another switch inside and a second door slid shut behind the first.

"You can relax now," he finally said. "No one knows of this place."

The quick walk had Sandy out of breath, but she managed to answer, "I'll be fine...just fine."

Suddenly he was conscious of her perfume. He hadn't bothered to turn on the light yet, but she was standing close to him now, and for the first time he realized how lonely he had been since he came to Saratoga. Now he flicked the switch on a small night light and his eyes shifted to Sandy's face.

Then the second shock of the day hit him. "Sweet Jesus," he uttered, recognizing her. Sandy's eyes narrowed, then widened, almost in the same instant. "The girl from *Lillian's*," he said.

Sandy nodded.

"And what do I do with you now?"

"Pardon me," she said wearily. "This wasn't exactly my idea."

Flint laughed. "No, I guess you're right. It's just that I'm not used to playing nursemaid at

118

this stage in my life."

"If I wasn't scared half to death, I'd let you off the hook," said Sandy. "But right now, I'm scared as hell. You wouldn't have a drink in this place, would you?"

"There's booze upstairs," he replied. "It's also my living quarters."

"I can't believe it," she said. "They say this place has been vacant for years."

"I hope for your sake and mine, they keep thinking that," said Flint. "Be careful and follow me up these stairs."

Sandy was surprised at the modern apartment housed within the upper floor of the mansion. Flint showed her around, pointing out his communication equipment with pride and, though he didn't think she was all that interested, the assortment of weapons Harry had supplied him with.

"These are the tools of my trade," he said, sounding a bit sardonic.

"You have a small arsenal here," she remarked. "Isn't it against the law?"

"That's a good question," he replied.

He opened a cabinet and displayed several bottles of liquor. "What'll it be? I have a little of everything here."

"Scotch and water will be fine."

He watched her out of the corner of one eye while he poured the drinks. She slipped out of her coat and stood near the counter in a pair of tight-fitting dark slacks and a rich-looking grey wool sweater. Her dark hair was hanging straight down over her shoulders, and it glistened.

She looked absolutely ravishing, he thought, much more so than her mother at that age. He handed her the drink and offered a seat at the table.

It was an awkward situation for Flint. He really

didn't know whether to tell her who he was. She sipped her drink while he rushed his down. He was on his second while she hadn't quite finished half of hers. He could see that she wasn't really a drinker.

He toyed with his second drink so she could catch up with him.

"It's funny," she said. "My girl friend and I were talking about you the other day."

"What girl friend?"

"Why, Ellen, my friend at *Lillian's*."

"Oh, yes, I remember. Why did she think of me?"

"I don't know. We were just talking, and for some reason you came to mind."

"I must have made quite an impression that evening." "Sort of. But neither of us remembered your name."

He smiled."There goes my big ego."

She was staring at the cut on his cheek and the dried blood stuck to his hair. "Does your head still ache?"

"Somewhat. I was slightly dizzy in the car. It comes and goes."

"I have gauze and peroxide in my bag; let me dress it for you."

"Don't bother."

"Please. I'm a nurse. It should be cleaned."

"Don't worry. I've had lots of cuts."

She took the gauze out of her bag anyway and wet it with peroxide. Moving to his side, she began gently to remove the blood from his hair. "Your sweater's a mess," she insisted. "Take it off before I clean the face wound."

He glanced up at her. "Why, we hardly know each other, and already you're trying to undress me," he kidded.

"It's all on a professional level," she quickly replied.

He felt a sharp pain as the sweater, its collar quite tight, slipped over his head.

There was no hesitation in her movements. She cleaned the upper part of the cut, taking care not to open it any further. When the wound was dressed, she reached in her handbag and took out a small bottle of shampoo. "You'll have to move to the sink so I can wash out your hair," she said.

"You make me feel like a kid," he snorted.

"My grandmother always said men were nothing more than grown kids."

"I've heard that one before," he quipped.

"It won't take but a minute."

"If you insist!"

He felt the smooth fingers glide through his hair as she worked in the warm lather, aware of her gentle touch and her body pressed next to his as she leaned over to complete the rinsing. Although the cut stung, he was enjoying every minute of it. When she was done, she mopped his forehead and dried his hair with a towel.

"You're spoiling me," said Flint.

"No," she replied. "Someone spoiled you a long time ago."

" How can you tell?"

"Call it woman's intuition," she answered simply.

He went to the counter when she was done and poured himself another Scotch, adding just a touch of water to cut its bite.

"Do you care for another?" he asked, holding the bottle out in a gesture.

She shook her head. "I've had my limit, thank you."

"Then I'll have one for you," he said, seating himself once more at the table. She sat down across from him and for a long minute they stared at each other, he noticing again the dark delicate features that so much resembled her mother's yet were so much more beautiful. He couldn't bring himself to tell her about it. He knew he would eventually have to approach the subject, but he just couldn't now.

Her eyes grew serious and, reaching into her handbag, she took out a key and set it on the table. "This could be very important, I think."

"Whose is it?"

Her voice dropped, and for the first time since they arrived at the mansion, it almost broke into a sob. "Rob...Robin left it for me!"

Flint leaned forward and picked up the key. He noticed it was numbered. "When? Left it when?"

"The day before she died. She came to the hospital but I wasn't on duty. She left it with Tom Benson. He works at the hospital."

His face took on a dull, blank expression. "Who exactly is Benson?"

"I told you, he works at the hospital."

"In what capacity?"

"He's a day janitor."

Flint jumped up and moved again to the counter and filled his glass with more Scotch. "I think I'm past my limit too," he said.
"But something tells me I'll need this drink." He stopped and looked back at her. "Let's take this whole thing from the top and work down. How well do you know this Benson?"

"We're friends. Just good friends."

"Real close?"

Her eyes flared up at him. "Close like friends. Nothing more."

Flint was leaning with his back against the counter. "I'm not trying to get personal. I'm trying to help in the only way I know how, and that's asking lots of questions, no matter how trivial they may seem."

Sandy grabbed her empty glass. "If you don't mind, I'll have that second drink," she said, not looking up.

He went a little heavier on the Scotch this time.

"Shall we continue?" he said, handing her the drink.

"Benson's not what you think," she said mildly. "He's been retarded since a child. He has no immediate family as far as I know. I cheer him up whenever I can. He doesn't have the slightest idea what's taking place...except...except that he's aware Robin's dead."

"This looks like a locker key of some kind."

"It is," she replied. "Robin's note said it's a locker in the Greyhound terminal."

He flipped the key up and down in his right hand. "Does your friend Benson know this key number?"

"I'm not really sure."

"We must be sure," he said sharply.

"I'll call him," said Sandy.

"Fine," said Flint. "Then we'll all be in trouble."

She suddenly realized the gravity of Flint's questions. "I'm...I'm not good at this game," she said dryly. "I suppose Benson is in danger because of all this?"

"It's unlikely they would know anything about Benson," said Flint. "Unless his name popped up in general conversation with Robin at one time or another. Did she know him very well?"

"No," she replied. "I believe she only met him once...that is, once before the day she gave him the note. However, she might have met him on other occasions. After all, Saratoga is a small town."

"What's his address?" asked Flint.

"Ninety-five West Street. He lives on the first floor, rear apartment."

Flint finished the last of his drink and filled the glass this time with plain water.

After a time he said, "I'm going out again. I'll be doing some quick zigzagging around town, so I want you to stay put. There's a bed in there and you're welcome to it. I'll try to be back soon."

"Can I go with you?"

"Not on your life," he snapped. "I got you this far, we won't press our luck."

There was a worried expression on her face and Flint could almost anticipate her next question. However, he spoke first. "Don't worry. I'll be back. I'll check on Benson and secure that material in the locker, whatever it is. But just to set your mind at ease, I'll send a message to my friend Harry in New York. He'll come running if anything happens to me."

"I guess I'm really beginning to get frightened," said Sandy.

Flint smiled. "Me too, my dear. Even Flint gets frightened. Do as I say. Stay here. Go to bed and if it's anything that can't wait, I'll wake you when I get back. If not, I'll let you sleep till morning." He slipped on a shoulder holster and tucked a thin, smooth black pistol into it, covering it with a short leather jacket. He hesitated at the door before going out. "Promise me you'll go to sleep?"

She was beginning to feel the effect of the two Scotches and she actually was quite tired. She reached out and touched his arm. "Thanks, Flint. Please be careful."

There was an urge within her to kiss him, but she held back. He leaned over, kissed her forehead, and before she could respond, he went out the door and down the stairs.

10. How Very Beautiful

D octor Blake hadn't been contacted since Flint departed for Sandy's apartment, and he was now becoming apprehensive over the whole situation.

"Let's hope," he thought, "I did the right thing giving Flint her address."

Blake tried several times to call the apartment, but got no answer.

He had to take Flint seriously, for that look on Flint's face as he went out of the door of the office had said it all.

He looked at his watch. It was now past 10:30. Blake hadn't stayed this late in his office in several months. He toyed with some case records just to pass the time, but couldn't concentrate on what he was reading. He went to his desk and took out Robin's file. He had only seen her professionally on three visits, and the file wasn't very large, but he remembered those visits clearly.

Ever since she had first come to him -- somewhat in a dither -- he had felt a sympathy not felt for his other patients and a determination to get to the bottom of her troubles. And now, here in print and in fine-lined pencil notes he had personally taken down, shone clear the mixed-up little world that Robin had drifted through.

Robin was prone to telling only half-truths; he knew that after her first visit. Still he was able to extract enough to begin the slow -- sometimes painful -- mental unraveling that he thought would one day uncover her real problems.

Her sudden death had made it impossible.

He ran his index finger along the lines, reading slowly. He noted that she could, in spite of her troubles, manage at times to muster up false cheer. Someone far back had taken a bright, cheerful child and had turned her inside out. Blake wasn't quite sure whether it began with her husband, or perhaps in her adolescence. He was trying to discover the source when she died, and he knew now that this mournful question would never be answered.

She lived on welfare money, so she said, but Blake also knew that she had other income, though probably not very substantial. She took drugs also, but he surmised that she was not totally addicted...she used them mostly to settle her nerves.

Things always seemed to get more complicated when he got into the area of what she did with her time. Robin could make up a thousand excuses about her daily and nightly habits, but this was where the half-truths came into play.

She once mentioned to Blake that she did some sort of research for a company downstate, but that it wasn't steady work, and furthermore, not important.

He had especially marked this in his notes, for he felt it had a lot to do with her present condition. He had hoped she would open up more on this subject at later meetings ... meetings that never took place.

She talked very little of her child or her parents. Only once did she mention her husband. He had beaten her and he drank all the time.

She had a court order mandating that he not see her or the child.

Blake particularly noticed that she didn't have any close friends, save for Sandy, whom she mentioned on her visits but in reality didn't know very well either.

He glanced over the balance of the notes, trying to pick out many of her irrelevant remarks, hoping that some of them might link together -- none did. It was a delicate puzzle he wasn't able to piece together.

His desk buzzer rang. It was the operator. "You're still there, Doctor?"

"Yes," he replied. "I'm working late."

"There's a phone call for you," she said. "They didn't say who."

"Never mind," he snapped. "Put them through."

"I can't, Doctor. They called on the pay phone in the hall."

Blake felt that it must be Flint. He raced from his office and practically vaulted the twenty feet to the hall phone to the startled amazement of two passing nurses.

"It's just got to be you, Flint."

"It's me, Doc. We're all in one piece."

"Where is Sandy?" asked Blake.

"Tucked away safe and sound at the moment," said Flint.

"You're sure everything is all right?" insisted Blake.

"In this business, nothing is all right, Doc. But we're safe for now...." Then adding, "I've a favor to ask of you, Doc."

"What is it?"

"It concerns one very dead man," said Flint flatly. "He's laying very peacefully in Sandy's basement for now, but if someone discovers him in the next 24 hours, things might not remain so peaceful."

Blake was shocked by Flint's statement. "I thought you said everything went all right?"

"No, Doc, safe," Flint said. "There's a big difference."

"Then you want me to contact the police?" asked Blake.

"Not at all," said Flint. "I want to get that corpse out of that apartment building without anyone but you and me knowing about it."

"That's impossible," said Blake. "We have to report this. The coroner will have to get involved."

"Forget the coroner and the police," Flint yelled. "I need some time to cover my tracks and to get Sandy out of Saratoga while she's still alive and breathing. This stiff came to kill her, don't you understand, and there's more where he came from. Besides, I have to leave town on other business tonight, which isn't helping my time schedule...now figure something out. Make it look as if you're taking a sick person to the hospital, but get my dead friend out of that basement!"

"I'm not sure I can arrange this...this..."

"You must!" insisted Flint. "One more thing, there was some information in a locker that I retrieved earlier tonight. It's a note Robin left for Sandy. She refers to one Marty Dresser. Could this be the name of one of your patients?"

"No. No, I don't recall the name," said Blake. "Is there any information on this person?"

"It's a screwy note, Doc. Her handwriting isn't very clear and it almost looks as if she scribbled it on the run. She makes mention of dope, land, and Yaddo, but I don't get the whole drift."

"Did you say Yaddo?" asked Blake.

"Yes."

"That's out past the race track. It's the old Spencer Trask estate where writers and artists work."

"Do you know anyone there?" Flint asked.

"One of our hospital directors is also a director at *Yaddo*."

"Fine," said Flint. "See if you can get any information on this Dresser. I'll get back in touch with you soon. And one more thing, Doc. Say nothing to anyone about our meeting, your knowledge of Sandy's whereabouts or the fact that this Marty Dresser's name came up. As for Sandy, you'll be asked by some of the nurses or doctors, no doubt, so you might as well make up the best story you can think of at the moment -- that she took a leave of absence, or heard about another job in Boston. We'll be on the move for the next few days. I'll contact you personally or have someone else contact you. Everything should work out, I hope. Don't forget my dead pal, he's most likely turning rancid by now...cheers!"

Blake set down the phone in slow motion. He pinched himself, just to make certain he wasn't dreaming. He had seen men like this in movies and read about them in books, but actually having encountered one was a numbing experience. Flint talked about these things as if he were skipping down to the corner store to buy a coke. The cold indifference shocked Blake. Yet he knew Flint was a totally sane, rational man.

Back in his office Blake sat down to think things out. The prospect of trying to remove a corpse undetected from Sandy's place scared him. Not to mention the moral and ethical problems it posed for someone of his profession.

Besides, he would need help. Then he thought of Benson. Yes, Benson. If anyone would be willing to foster a cause to help Sandy, Benson would be the one.

It was raining outside Saratoga Hospital when Blake finally left for the night. The wind had picked up and everything seemed misty. Even the street lights appeared to take on an eerie glow.

Flint had also put in a long evening. As he drove along Union Avenue he couldn't help but notice the long line of mid-Georgian mansions in which so many expensive dinner parties and upper society functions had taken place over the years. The mansions appeared like great stone fortresses against the cold gray night, but he knew the wealthy owners would be here before long for the racing season, and that this assembly would bring along their well-planned and well-attended celebrations.

And somewhere mixed in with the real bluebloods would be the silent mobsters, so poised in their well-tailored dark suits that they could drift amid the elegance and gaiety of Saratoga's summer elite like strait-laced businessmen.

Flint had seen them do this in so many places around the world. Oh, the really wealthy still tried to shun them whenever possible, but there was no end to their quiet, persistent presence.

Now that so many rich children were into drugs of one sort or another, and quite a few of the parents as well, mob operatives moved easily among them. And, as members themselves of the newly rich society -- riches mostly obtained via drug traffic -- most of them were into buying horses.

Flint had changed his mind about keeping his appointment with Morin. He'd made contact with him and told him he'd be coming a day late. He wanted to catch some sleep, then make arrangements to get Sandy out of Saratoga. He also wanted to check out this Marty Dresser. He took his usual precautions, making his way home via back streets and slipping into his place as quietly as possible. Sandy was sleeping in his bed.

The door to the room was ajar, and he could hear her quiet breathing.

He decided to sleep on the small divan in the outer room. Outside the March wind grew stronger. He dozed off once, then woke to a sudden noise. It was only a tree limb hitting the side of the building. He went back to sleep. He woke again to a movement in the room. He sat up quickly, automatically reaching for his gun.

"Flint, are you there?" Her voice sounded scared.

He turned on the light. Sandy stood shivering at the bedroom door. "I had a terrible dream," she said. "I guess this is all catching up to me."

She was clad in a short blue nightgown. It cut off just at her knees. She leaned back against the door casing, letting her hands fall loosely to her sides.

"I'm just not cut out for this," she said with an exasperated sigh.

"Would you care for a cigarette?" he asked. "I'd love one."

He moved over on the divan and she sat next to him without being asked. He lit their cigarettes. He looked at her closely, noting the thick dark hair, with soft natural waves. Her eyes and nose were so perfectly shaped that he couldn't believe it. Sandy's hand shook slightly. "Just look at me," she said. "I'm a nervous wreck about this."

"It's quite natural," Flint replied. "It's not every day you get involved in a killing."

"Oh, that...that man. Who do you think he was?"

Flint thought for a moment. "I wish I knew. He could have been working for any number of people. I wish I knew who sent him."

She then turned to face him. "Who do you work for, Flint?"

"Myself."

"I'm serious. Who do you work for?" she insisted.

He reached out and took her right hand gently in his. She didn't resist or approve of the action, and he looked her straight in the eye. "I'd like to tell you everything, my dear, but it could prove dangerous to you in the future. Let's just say I'm a guy doing a job. If I find the right time and place, I'll tell you all about it."

"I guess I'm talking too much," she said. "Look. You risked your life for me today. It could have been you lying in the basement.
I'm grateful you came along. I'll get back to sleep now if I can."

Then, without hesitation, she leaned forward and kissed him. She held it for a moment, then drew back.

He said nothing. She stood up and went back into the bedroom, this time closing the door. He lay awake for a long time, the taste of her lipstick fresh upon his lips.

Later he heard her stirring restlessly. Then she called out. He went into the room and found her sitting up in bed. She was shivering again.

"Shall I stay with you?" he asked.

She nodded. Flint slipped beneath the covers beside her. She lay quietly, her breathing now relaxed. He ran his strong hand down her shoulder, stopping at her waist. She rose up slowly as he wrapped his arm around her, the full length of her body coming next to his. Her long dark hair fell over her face and shoulders as she buried her face in his chest and kissed him on the neck. She no longer was shivering. She kissed him for a long while when it was over, and then fell into a deep sleep.

Flint stayed awake watching her. At first he felt guilty. He hadn't expected it would lead to this so quickly, but the feeling of guilt soon left him.

It had all been so natural and marvelous. "How beautiful you are," he whispered to himself. "How very beautiful!"

He removed his arm from under her head and replaced it with a pillow.

The wind was howling now outside in the cold Saratoga early morning hours, and eventually Flint dropped off to sleep while listening to the wind and Sandy's soft breathing.

11. See You In L.A.

F lint and Sandy slipped out of Saratoga the next morning, surprisingly without incident. Flint had contacted Harry Waite and arrangements were made to have a private plane meet them at the Warren County airport, just south of Lake George in the Adirondacks. Flint planned to have the plane drop him off in Quebec so he could keep his appointment with Morin, and then take Sandy to Boston where she would catch a commercial flight to L.A. He figured that would be the safest place for her for the time being.

Neither had eaten breakfast and they were ravenously hungry. He pulled into a small diner along the way and they ordered bacon and eggs. Again, it was a case of too much happening too quickly, and Flint hadn't had time to phone Monica in L.A. -- Monica being his first choice to look after Sandy until things calmed down.

During breakfast he excused himself to make a long distance call. He tried reaching her at home, but there was no answer; he then had the call placed to her studio in Burbank.

"Well," said Monica, on answering his call. "My long lost man has finally come home."

"No," said Flint. "I'm not home."

"Where are you?"

"Far away from all that lovely sunshine you're probably enjoying. And that's all I can tell you right now."

"You have your nerve," Monica cried. "You up and take off and don't even tell anyone you're going. Besides, we had a date. Remember?"

"We did, and you're right," he admitted. "But things don't always go as planned for me. You should be used to it by now."

"I'll never understand you and I'll never get used to it," said Monica. "So why even bother to call me?"

"Now don't go getting out of control, my dear. It can all be explained."

"I should just hang up...I think I will," she blared over the phone.

"Please don't do that," he said slowly.

"And why not?" Monica asked.

"Because there are two lives on the line, and one is mine."

"Jesus, Flint," Monica begged. "Why don't you get the hell out of that rotten business?"

"I just might," he said agreeably. "But I have to get through this mess first." Then kidding her, "Perhaps I'll take up acting. Can you use a good leading man?"

"You're beginning to scare me," said Monica. "What's this call all about, anyway?"

"I want you to watch over a girl. I'll be sending her to L.A. sometime this evening. She's in great danger here, but I don't think this danger will follow her to the coast. Anyway, will you put her up for a few days?"

There was a long pause, then Monica spoke. "You're not asking me to babysit some kid, are you?"

"She's over twenty, Monica. She can babysit herself."

"Look," Monica pleaded. "I'll help you out, but

136

you must realize I have a busy schedule. Who'll keep her company in the meantime?"

"She'll read lots of books and watch lots of TV," said Flint. "The important thing is that you keep it all quiet. Go about your work, but don't mention that she's staying with you."

"Hell, Flint. You never make it easy, do you? Send her out, I'll do my best."

"Thanks, Mon...I'll call you tomorrow to make certain she arrived safe."

"When will I see you, Flint?" Monica asked with a touch of sadness in her voice.

"Very soon, my dear. Very soon. She'll be arriving on United Air, Flight 330 into L.A. International. Her name is Sandy Blair. She's a brunette, pretty face..."

"Don't tell..." Monica interjected. "She's young and beautiful."

"Yes. I guess you could say that."

"How well do you know her?" Monica asked.

"I won't discuss that right now," he replied. "You're a peach for helping me out. Stay beautiful, and I'll see you sometime soon."

Flint put down the phone and returned to the table. "I've got you set with a close friend in L.A. I'll fill you in on the way to the plane."

They finished eating and he paid the check. On the way to the airport he gave her detailed instructions about keeping a very low profile while in California -- in fact, not showing her face at all until he contacted her again.

Within minutes of reaching the Warren County airport, a small sleek twin-engine Piper appeared in the blue sky overhead, dipped its wings, swung low over the field and made a quick landing.

Flint, ignoring a *"Do Not Pass"* sign, drove out on the landing strip, and with the pilot's help, transferred what little baggage they had from the car to the plane. He put Sandy aboard, went to park the car at the far end of the terminal parking lot, and ran out and hopped in just as the pilot gunned the engines. The pilot cleared with the tower for take-off, pushed the stick and with a jerk the plane moved forward, headed down the runway and lifted smoothly into the air within a few hundred feet. He turned north, flying just above the peaks of the Adirondacks, across a wide stretch of Lake George, and levelling off, pointed the plane's nose toward Quebec.

Shortly over an hour later the Piper was circling the Quebec airport. The plane had to wait five minutes before landing, so they cruised a mile or two from the strip, taking in the crystal clear view of the old city and the winding, majestic St. Lawrence River in the distance.

Finally the pilot brought the plane in, setting down so lightly that there wasn't the slightest bump.

"I'll get out near the terminal," said Flint, glancing at Sandy as he said it. "Don't go too close. I want you off the ground immediately after I'm out."

Sandy clasped his hand in hers. "I want to stay with you, Flint."

"No, that's impossible. Go to L.A. where it's safe!"

"Be careful, Flint," she said, her voice beginning to break and a tear forming on her cheek.

"I'll be OK, don't worry." He said it without looking at her. Then he turned toward her and she fell into his arms sobbing. He held her for a moment, kissed her and held her closer. The pilot tried to ignore the encounter.

Flint released her. "I must go. You must go. I will see you in L.A....that's a date."

The pilot signaled it was time for take-off.

Flint jumped out, pulling his belongings with him. He leaned inside the doorway once more and kissed her again, then shut the door.

The plane's engines suddenly roared and a spray of fine snow swirled near its tail as it began slowly to move away. It picked up speed and headed down the runway and lifted into the sky. Flint remained standing on the edge of the runway, his bags in hand, and watched as it circled back and passed across the field. It was but a few hundred feet overhead and he could plainly see Sandy waving. He continued to wave until the plane went out of sight. It was then he had the afterthought that maybe he should have kept her in Quebec.

12. A Brass Band

Old Quebec had not changed. Oh, there were a few new high-rise hotels dotting the sky line that Flint hadn't seen before, but for the most part, the city still possessed quaintness, charm, and was filled with excellent French-style restaurants. He had always referred to it as the "Paris of North America" and he wondered if its inhabitants -- mostly of French descent -- were still carrying on their staunch battle to separate from Canada proper.

As he drove east along the Avenue Ste. Anne he noted the numerous cafe signs, the many narrow side streets where artists hung their paintings, and directly ahead, standing by itself against the bright, clear sky, the imposing spires and walls of the Chateau Frontenac.

He parked his rented car near the big hotel, but didn't go directly inside. Instead, he headed for a small cafe nearby called the Ripaille, where he sat down in one of the chairs near the door and ordered a glass of white wine. He sipped his wine and waited patiently for Morin.

Eventually a short, gray-haired man with a thin face poked his head inside the cafe entrance, his rather large round eyes glancing around the room until they came to rest on Flint. The man looked cautiously over his shoulder, then stepped inside. He nodded toward Flint and slid into a chair at the next table, his back half-turned to Flint. The waiter, a rueful expression on his face, came over to take his order. The man ordered soda water with ice.

When the waiter was gone, Flint asked, "Are you Morin?"

Turning slowly, the man looked at him. "Par-don, monsieur. You must be Father O'Malley?"

Flint touched the white collar that showed against his black suit and brushed his fingers over his dark mustache. He was wearing a black hat and horn-rimmed glasses which he adjusted as he stared into the thin face. "Yes, I am Father O'Malley," he insisted with a smile.

"So you've come to Quebec to see our beautiful churches, Father? Yes, we have many outstanding churches. You won't want to miss the magnificent paintings, either. Very old. Very much old Quebec." His nostrils dilated, and he forced back a smile as he continued to speak. "And, may I say, enjoy the best eating in the world. We have the best innkeepers, and most meals are `modique,' very inexpensive."

He then lowered his voice and moved his chair closer, whispering, "Word on the street says St. Jacques knows you're coming to Quebec...I don't know how he knows, but he knows. I had nothing to do with this, I assure you. There's a leak somewhere in your organization...perhaps right in New York. I'm certain of it."

He was about to continue when a female patron came into the cafe. She seated herself at a far table. Morin looked in her direction.

"Good afternoon, mademoiselle." He said it softly to see if his voice was carrying across the room. She didn't seem to hear him clearly, though she blushed and nodded back. He then went on to address Flint. Flint sat up straight. He didn't particularly like what he had heard, and he didn't quite know what to make of Morin's frankness. Harry Waite's description of him wasn't exactly true, either. He could believe Morin or not. If it were a

142

setup, he could be putting his head on the block. "My God," he thought. "There were lots of severed heads lying beneath the ruins of this old city!" He didn't want to join this select crowd. Not just yet. He tested the waters with Morin, asking, "You're not very fond of Harry, are you?"

"I've never liked him," Morin admitted. "I've also never crossed him. He's cheap and we don't really get along, but I've always played it square with Harry. However, I like to get paid well for my work...I take lots of risks."

Flint was listening closely. "You just might know where the leak is coming from," Flint prophesied. "Do you?"

"No, I don't. I can't help you there."

"Not even a speculation?" asked Flint.

Morin's thin face wore a wide smile. "Maybe it's Harry?"

"I'll rule that one out," replied Flint.

" So many places these leaks can come from," Morin sighed. "Money talks. Even the best cops will betray friends if the price is right." Then his eyes lit up and he suddenly appeared to have the answer....

Flint anticipated it, leaned forward. "Tell me Morin, who is it?."

"No. No. I don't know. I can only guess, and it's not fair to guess on such grave things. No fair to single out anyone unless I know for certain."

"You had someone in mind," insisted Flint. "Let me be the judge. Give me the name."

"It's only my intuition," said Morin squinting his eyes. "If I come up with a name it doesn't mean anything. I have no evidence nor basis to single out anyone at this point. As I say, I go with my intuition. Logic, however, tells me it's someone very close to Harry. Could it be Georgio?"

Flint dismissed this theory. "You must have more faith in the people you work with," Flint said. "Harry runs a tight ship. He knows his associates implic- itly."

Morin bent his head toward the table as the waiter came back to see if they wanted another drink. When he left, Morin spoke again. "We haven't much time and there are a few things I think you should know before you get too involved up here." He looked cautiously again toward the doorway and at the waiter across the room, as if to be certain they wouldn't be overheard. Then, turning further around, he gave Flint an impatient glance.

"The Saratoga thing between the Quebec and New York families has been settled. It involves drugs and horses. They've got a few jockeys on the take, but any race fixing is very selective. My point is this. There isn't any so-called war going on. St. Jacques made a deal. He gets his cut and New York gets theirs. He's given a piece of the local action to one of the New Jersey mobs, so they stay out of it too."

"It sounds too simple," whispered Flint.

"It is," said Morin. "They both know the Feds are watching the situation closely. War at this time makes them both losers. They've got no choice. Any open conflict at this stage would be useless to both organizations."

"What about the girl?" asked Flint. "Which family killed her?"

Morin smiled back coldly. "You take such risks for one little girl...I'm surprised," said Morin.

"You didn't answer my question," demanded Flint.

"Well, for one thing, you won't appreciate my answer," said Morin, shrugging his shoulders.

"Try me," said Flint.

"No one knows. They're all baffled. She didn't know anything, anyway. We can't figure it out."

"You're positive?" asked Flint.

"I've talked to some very reliable people. They say they're also looking into it. They don't know."

"It's something I'd like to forget about," said Flint, "but I can't. By the way, does the name Marty mean anything to you?"

"Never heard of him."

Flint's voice became more serious. "What do your reliable people say about the guy who tried to axe me in Saratoga? Or have I shocked you with this one?"

"I didn't know," replied Morin, his thin face troubled. "There's been no mention of it."

"Quite so," continued Flint. "Yeah, he knew his business, too. Why, I walked right into that one. I guess I must be slipping."

Morin toyed with his soda water, clicking the ice with his finger. "Look, Flint, we must make this visit as brief as possible. I'll see what I can find out about this Marty and the bum who tried to take you out. There's nothing worth staying in Quebec for. St. Jacques won't bother you unless you start making waves. Get back to Saratoga and let things up here rest. It's not your fight -- in fact, there's no basis for you staying around."

"Perhaps you're correct, Morin. But I really can't leave now without finding out who tipped St. Jacques off about my arrival, can I?"

"Do you think he'll tell you who it was?" asked Morin.

"That all depends," said Flint.

The waiter returned to take another order. Morin waved him off. He reached in his pocket and took out some money and laid it on the table. "I must be going, my friend. Persist if you must, but remember that there won't be anyone to lean on if the going gets rough. You're very deep in the wrong territory. There aren't any bridges to cross back over."

Morin was about to rise when the woman across the room got up and walked to the door. The bright afternoon sun glared through the entrance as she opened the door, and in that instant, Morin, always alert to people around him, recognized her. He turned to Flint when she had left. "My God, I know that woman!"

"Who is she?" Flint blurted.

"She works undercover for the Provincial government. I don't know her name. I'm positive of her position, though."

"That's great," Flint sighed. "I could have come to town with a brass band and drawn less attention."

"Don't worry about it," said Morin, thinking it over. "I believe the timing was purely coincidental. She doesn't know me, and you look more like a priest than my pastor...we -- you -- we all tend to get jittery in this business, don't we?"

"No comment," added Flint.

"I will be going now," Morin said. "You'll no doubt stay the night but, as I suggest, go back to Saratoga tomorrow. Please?"

He moved away from the table and went out the door without so much as a glance back at Flint.

Flint paid his bill and left shortly thereafter, going directly to the Chateau.

At the Chateau he parked in the outer parking lot and walked the long driveway to the portico leading to the main lobby. Once inside he could hardly believe his eyes. Major renovation had taken place since he was last there and the modern appearance seemed a sharp contrast to the Chateau's austere exterior of gray stone. New carpets had been installed and the walls sparkled with bright embroidered tapestries.The rigid furnishings of yesteryear had been replaced with an assortment of rich, smart-looking divans and chairs, all well placed so that the traffic flow moved easily about the lobby.

Flint checked in at the main desk, signing the register as Father Edward O'Malley of St. Mary's Parish, Daytona Beach, Florida. He was still sporting a California tan which his disguise couldn't hide, so he used the Florida address to give some credibility for looking so healthy.

He was assigned room 203, overlooking the St. Lawrence River and, as Flint observed on first entering the large room with double bed, his window looked down on the old section of town and just above the point where a tram car on tracks was located; this was used to transport tourists to the Chateau. He observed further that his window was some fifty feet above the top of the tram car and another hundred feet or so above the base of the great Chateau wall. He reckoned it would make for an impossible escape route should he need one.

He was beginning to feel the weariness of the last few days, so he decided to rest for an hour or two before making any set plans to return to Saratoga. He was not sure about Morin, yet based on their short meeting, he decided to trust him. His mind raced on about many things and at first he couldn't doze off, but eventually he did sleep soundly.

He was dreaming one of his weird dreams when the telephone rang. He popped open his eyes and reached for the receiver. It was near sundown, and streaks of amber light shone through the window, spreading a soft glow across the room.

"Pardon, Father O'Malley," a thickly accented voice said, "there's a message for you."

"Yes. Yes. Who is it from?" he asked.

"Monsieur Morin called. He said it is important that you meet him tonight. He left an address."

He was feeling lightheaded from his nap. "Let me have the address," he said curtly.

"You're to meet Monsieur Morin at the *Traite du Roy*. It is located on the Rue Notre Dame in the old section. He'll be there about 9 o'clock. Meet him outside."

Flint checked his watch. It was not yet seven. "Thank you," he said, setting the phone down.

He then reached for the phone again and placed a call to Harry Waite, using a special coded conversation Central had worked out for just such calls. Harry wasn't available, so Flint dictated his message to a tape recorder. He forwarded the address of the *Traite du Roy* and his scheduled meeting

147

with Morin. He closed by saying that he was going to try some authentic "Frog" food.

He lay back down. Suddenly all his thoughts turned to Sandy. He guessed that her plane would be somewhere over the West by now, flying safely to meet Monica.

He wanted her very much at this moment. He also knew that one day shortly he would have to tell her everything. He wondered what her reaction would be. He also knew that some time in the future he would have to reconcile his involvement with Sandy with her mother. He wasn't looking forward to this encounter, but he knew it was inevitable.

He dozed off again and when he finally awoke it was raining outside his window. It wasn't a heavy downpour, but it was steady. He went to the window, opened it and peered out. A fine mist was blowing in swirls along the side of the hotel and visibility was reduced to a few hundred feet in any direction.

He checked the time again. It was exactly 8:30. He dressed in the same priest outfit, also putting on a light-weight vinyl all-weather coat, and left the Chateau for his rendezvous with Morin.

13. My Calling Card, Monsieur?

Flint rode the tram car to the bottom of the wall, hanging tightly to the handrail as it jerked its way down the steep pitch. The *Traite du Roy* was a short walk from the tram, however; the wind had now picked up and the mist became rain again. He wore leather-soled shoes which proved to be a poor choice, as the narrow streets of the old section were paved with cobblestones and extremely slippery. It was like walking on ice cubes.

On the way the question kept bothering him, "Why had Morin called so soon?" Perhaps Morin had more to say about the Quebec connection, or perhaps he had some additional information on Robin. It was a risk Flint figured he had to take, but his instinct still told him Morin could be trusted.

He reached the cafe and took what protection he could find under a small canopy over its entrance. There was no sign of Morin. A taxi pulled up in front and a young couple hurried inside, the man sheltering the girl from the rain with a trench coat. Another car arrived and this time two couples stepped out. They apparently had been drinking elsewhere and all were quite drunk. One of the men slipped as he closed the car door. They all laughed as he picked himself up, dripping wet and swearing in French. Laughing louder, they all stumbled through the entranceway.

A strong wind was now coming in off the St. Lawrence, blowing rain into Flint's face. He checked his watch; it was 9:10. "To hell with this," he whispered to himself, "I'm going inside."

He turned toward the door, but didn't quite make it. Two dark figures appeared to his right and left, and before he had time to move, his arms were pinned behind his back. They spun him around and he saw the dim running lights of a car as it pulled to the curb.

Flint made one last effort to break free by pushing his body upward, but a third figure came from behind and hit him in the back of the neck. It was the last thing he remembered.

He had no idea where he was nor what time it was. The smell of raw fish and vinegar filled his nostrils. He was half-seated on a hard bench in a small room with one light.

Faint voices could be heard outside the room. He was in an uncomfortable position on the bench, with his hands and feet bound. The only relief he could find was by leaning to one side, then the other. Yet even this was difficult and he feared falling off the bench if he leaned too far.

Suddenly the door opened and a young man, holding a gun in his right hand, came into the room. He was soon followed by four other men, all of husky build and dressed in dark overcoats and fedoras. They looked like mobsters, and they were. He'd seen many of them before. All dressed the same, standing before him like twentieth century clones.

The biggest of the bunch, a stout, red-faced character, grabbed Flint's hair and lifted his head so that he looked directly into the lone light.

"You like Quebec, Mr. Flint?" he asked in a garlic-laden, rough voice.

"Yes. It's beautiful this time of year."

The hand pulled his hair again hard, and he could feel several strands pop loose.

"Very quick with your mouth, I see, Mr. Flint."

He didn't reply this time.

They were interrupted by a sixth man who appeared in the doorway, his hugeness immediately apparent to Flint. He was over six feet tall and must have weighed well over three hundred pounds. The others stepped aside as he came closer to Flint.

"Shame. Shame. You come into my city when you're not invited," the huge man said. "Tourists are welcome to Quebec, snoopers are not."

Flint stared up at the hard, round face. He knew it was St. Jacques speaking.

"I want to tell you a few things, Mr. Flint. Then I'm going to give you some advice. It's up to you what you do with it." He motioned for a chair and one of his men brought one from a far corner of the room. He drew it up right in front of Flint. St. Jacques looked at the man holding Flint by the hair, and he let loose. Face to face, sitting at the same level, Flint felt dwarfish.

"Ah, yes," St. Jacques continued. "You come to Quebec and I know all about it. Now, you ask yourself, who told me? That's a good question. It was not Claude Morin. Morin is a little fish. We let little fish swim around. They lead us to big fish. They sometimes can be a bother, but Morin is no bother. Still, someone told me about your arrival. Naturally you will have to find this out for yourself. The real point is, why are you here, and why do you think I'm involved with whatever it is you're involved with? Advice! I have nothing to do with the matter you were hired to investigate. If I have business in Saratoga, it has

nothing to do with anything even remotely connected to your interest in a certain girl's death.
I'll say no more on this subject."

St. Jacques took out a leather case and
slipped a cigar into his mouth without lighting
it. "I would offer you one, Mr. Flint, but, as you
can imagine, I'm upset with you, so I won't.
Sometimes certain people use very cleverly designed diversions. You Americans often refer to
this as a smokescreen. Perhaps this is what you
should be looking for. The curtain behind the
curtain, so to speak. I will be leaving you now.
I'm sorry you insisted on coming this far. I'm sure
right now you realize it wasn't worth it."

He drifted upward from the chair, his hulk
expanding like a balloon inflating. "I won't bother
to leave my calling card. My men will take care
of that."

He stopped at the door and turned. "You may
also be wondering why I don't speak with an ac-
cent. Simple, I was born and educated in the
United States. Right over the border in Rouses
Point. However, I speak French, as well as two
other languages." His eyes once more surveyed
Flint. "Very stupide of you to come, Mr.
Flint,...very stupide!"

It was the sharp clinking sound of metal that
first woke him. He felt pains throughout his body,
mainly concentrated in his face and neck. He
tried to reach up but his arm was like lead. He
couldn't muster any mobility. Then he recalled
vaguely what had happened; how they had come
at him with fists flying, one of them using a billy
club against his ribs and back. He coughed and
pitched forward, breathing with great difficulty.
One or more ribs were broken, he was sure of
that. He hoped they wouldn't puncture his lungs.
They'd beaten his face and head so that his eyes

were but half open. Yes. They were a special breed and they were experts at this sort of thing; goons of the first order who actually delighted in their work.

The clinking noise became louder, and the place where he was seated suddenly began to move. It jerked once, then again, and in slow repeated jerks seemingly was taking him upward. It was dark and he couldn't make out where he was. The metallic banging hurt his ear drums, overly sensitive now because of the beating he had taken.

It was difficult even to think. The pain racking his whole body was almost unbearable.

He coughed again and experienced a shortage of breath that left him straining for air. It came in a succession of coughs. He lost consciousness.

When he again woke, a light was shining in his face. His eyes opened ever so slowly and the pale image of a man appeared. He was narrow-shouldered and thin-faced, and he was talking in intense, choppy sentences. Flint managed to blink open one eye, just long enough to recognize Morin.

"Ah, I knew this would happen. They get nasty over nothing. You didn't deserve this!" Then Morin, leaning over to observe Flint's condition further, let out a sigh. "It must have been LaDuke. It looks like his work. He's the worst of the lot in St. Jacques' family."

The swelling around Flint's mouth made it difficult to speak, but he managed to ask where they were.

"We're still inside the tram," said Morin. "When did they put you in here?"

"Don't know...know. Can't recall," Flint blurted out. Morin went about examining Flint's injuries intently. "Do your ribs hurt?"

Flint nodded his head.

"Then stay as still as you can," said Morin. "We must get help in moving you from here."

"I'm hurt very badly," said Flint in a deep-throated whisper.

"I know, my friend. I know. We will get help for you. Stay still and I'll go and get some assistance...I'll be back in five minutes."

It was still dark outside, and Flint had the feeling momentarily that he was bleeding to death internally.

"You will be fine, my friend," Morin reassured him.

Morin left and Flint was alone in the silence of the tram. He not only was hurt badly, he was very much confused. He knew it would take some time to get over this beating, perhaps weeks. St. Jacques had left his calling card all right. And somewhere within Central's structure there was a big leak...Flint now realized that someone in Central wanted him off this assignment. The question was, who? Both Harry and Morin were right, he shouldn't have pushed this too far in Quebec. But at least he was still alive and for some strange reason, St. Jacques had given him a new lease on life. For an even stranger reason St. Jacques had deliberately planted the seed that a third party might be involved. He probably would never know Morin's full involvement in the affair, but at this point he was thankful for his help.

His body was becoming chilled and the pain in his face increased. He wondered what time it was. Somewhere near morning, for now a gray light filled the sky. Short gusts of wind blew against the tram, shaking it and adding to his pain. He was about to cave in when the side door opened and Morin, followed by a large bearded man, climbed into the tram.

154

Flint groaned as they lifted him under the arms and started for the steps. The large man, breathing hard, gave him a sympathetic look, taking extra care not to grasp too close to his rib cage as he assisted Flint up the steps and into a waiting car.

The man drove and Morin sat in the back seat and held Flint's head with his left hand.

"This is Don LaDuke," said Morin. Then quickly adding, "No relation to the LaDuke with St. Jacques. He has a place where we can be safe and where we can treat you."

Flint didn't answer. He had dozed off the minute he was put into the car.

14. What Are Friends For?

The first thing he noticed was dazzling sun light making luminous signs across the ceiling and walls in the room where he lay in bed. He smelled fresh salt air, carried on a mild breeze into the room, and he could hear the endless change and struggle of the sea as it pitched against the rocks just below the open window. He realized he was in his own bedroom in Palos Verdes. He realized it without the slightest notion of how he arrived there from Quebec, nor how much time had elapsed.

The bedroom door opened and he caught a glimpse of blonde hair in the sunlight.

"Flint," Monica's familiar voice called softly. "Are you awake?"

"Yes," he replied. "I'm not sure this is real, that I'm alive."

She came over and sat on the edge of the bed. "You were a sorry sight when they brought you here."

He reached for her hand. "They? Who are they?"

"Oh, the two Canadians, Morin and LaDuke."

"They came all the way to California?"

"Yes. They stayed for two weeks. They wouldn't leave until the doctor was certain you'd make it through. They said you had lost consciousness for a two-day period after they found you. Apparently you were in worse shape than expected. They drove you to California in a van. You were in a coma all the way. Doctor Rubenstein, a neurosurgeon friend of mine, took care of you once here."

"Then I guessed right for once," he said.

"About what?"

"About Morin."

She brushed the hair from his forehead with soft fingers. "He was very concerned about you. He felt he was to blame. He said he shouldn't have let you out of his sight. I've never heard you mention his name. Do you know him well?"

"Funny you should ask," he said. "I never met him until I went to Quebec. Even at that, it was a short meeting. Someone using his name called the Chateau and I thought I was on my way to meet him. They...the mob boys grabbed me outside a cafe."

"Morin saved your life," Monica reflected. Her lips parted and he saw the bright smile and smooth white teeth. Then her voice dropped. "God! We thought you were going to die on us."

"Well, maybe for once I should have taken Harry's advice. He told me not to go to Quebec. Perhaps it wasn't all for nothing, though?"

She looked at him. "I know what you're thinking, Flint. Let me tell you right now, we're not letting you go back there."

"Did you ever know me to leave a job undone?"

"That's the trouble. You don't know when to stop. This one's gone too far already."

"It's not my nature to quit."

The color glowed in her cheeks. "You might consider the strain this puts on your friends. Besides, I've told you a hundred times, you're getting too old for this game."

"I suppose you're right," he said. "But I must wrap this case up, even if it means returning

158

East." Then in a sudden change of mood, he asked, "Where is Sandy? Has she been here since my return?"

"No," Monica said. "She begged to come and help, but I wasn't taking any chances. I've kept her isolated since her arrival in California. Not even my best friends know she's here. I knew you would have wanted it that way...you told me...."

"Christ, Mon," he interrupted, "what would I do without you?" Monica went to the open window and pulled aside the thin curtains.

"We've known each other a long time, Flint. Maybe too long, too well. Anyway, I've been hung up on you; you've got to know that. There were times when I even told myself that perhaps...just perhaps, we'd tie the knot. Would you believe, even a hard career-minded broad like Monica thinking about marriage? Sandy and I have become very close these past few weeks. She's too young for you, Mike, I keep telling myself, but the age difference won't deter her from loving you. She's an incredibly warm and sincere girl. If anyone is going to pin you down, it will be Sandy. You'd be a fool to let her slip by. You probably already know this. Why, the writers at the studio couldn't write a better script if they tried!"

There was a long silence between them. Flint finally spoke. "I'm grateful to you, Monica."

"Don't go getting soft on me," she insisted, her voice tightening. "That's what friends are for."

"You're more than a friend..." he didn't continue the sentence, for she went to the door.

"I've got a script to read. If you need anything, I'll be on the patio."

"Thanks," he said. "I'll try and catch some sleep."

Soon, the phone rang and Monica came in and woke him. Morin was calling from Saratoga.

"Here we go again," Monica said, handing him the cordless phone.

Morin's voice came over loud and clear. "Hey, they say you're doing fine," he said. "You had me worried, my friend."

"I never would have made it without you and whatzisname...LaDuke...yes, you and LaDuke. That mustta been an extraordinary trip across the States, with me lying in the van like a corpse?"

They both laughed.

"I'm sorry, my friend, for letting you get into that situation," said Morin. "By chance that evening I contacted Harry on another matter and he mentioned you were on your way to the cafe to meet me. It was then I felt sick inside. I knew someone had set you up."

"I've been concentrating on that angle," said Flint. "Someone in Central is leaking everything."

"I have thought this for a long time," exclaimed Morin. "And it may just tie into your close call here in Saratoga."

"What have you found out?" asked Flint.

"Several things," said Morin. "To begin with, your attacker came all the way from Colombia...Colombia, South America. Very little is known about him. He worked for a select group that specializes in contract killings. He was called the 'Grasshopper.' He was extremely good at the martial arts."

"How well I know," Flint interjected.

"Anyway, this outfit has carried out numerous contracts for the mob, both down South and around the East Coast. They've also been known to do private jobs if the price were right. The right person, knowing their operation, could hire them out for 25 or 30 thousand a contract. The mob pays them a flat 20 grand. They make it up in volume."

That's it," Flint said angrily. "He was after

Sandy. I just happened along at the right moment. He didn't have any idea of my involvement. He might even have thought I'd been hired to kill her."

"I don't understand," Morin said.

"I'll explain it all at another time," said Flint. "Fill me in on anything else you might have."

"I picked up some information on your Marty character. It's she, not he. It turns out that Marty is a feisty ex-college student who's been dope-ridden since she was a freshman. Her parents are dead, and she's heir apparent to the estate of her grandparents, who own land across the country, including land near the race track. She lives in a small cottage near Yaddo Park. She used to throw some real wild parties. My source says she's near crazy, but the local authorities haven't done anything about her as yet. She's got a lot of haphazard friends, and she's well supplied with dope, though they can't figure out where she's getting it all. She also places lots of long distance calls to New York City. Again, these can't be traced. She places them to different pay booths."

"We're getting closer," Flint remarked. "Robin's note mentioned Marty and Yaddo. If it's that heavy, Robin might have stumbled onto something big without realizing it."

"There's more," added Morin. "Marty's grandparents are both in nursing homes. The grandfather is close to dying, and the grandmother had a stroke last month and isn't expected to live out the year. This little pothead will be worth several million when they go. Can you imagine it?"

"I can imagine anything by now," Flint said. "Obviously there's a connection here somewhere. I have the feeling this Marty is the key to it, or at least a major link. Someone's after her money. Yeah, someone's after her money and the land."

"It seems to be pointing that way," agreed Morin. "Checking around Saratoga since you left, I find that big plans are in the making for a hotel convention center. The city council almost had things settled in downtown Saratoga, but somehow the original bid got thrown out. Then they started infighting throughout the county political apparatus. Marty's sitting on the next best choice for this complex. The land value will quadruple overnight if they elect to build in that direction."

Flint's excitement was growing. He wanted to jump out of bed and head for the airport. Everything was falling into place now; he could feel it in his blood. "If I weren't stuck here in Palos Verdes, I'd be in Saratoga tomorrow," he told Morin. He felt the muscles stiffen in his chest and the small dull pain as the bandages pulled on his injured ribs, reminding him just how badly he had been hurt.

"Don't rush things," warned Morin, sensing Flint's anxiety. "It's the beginning of July. We've got the whole summer ahead of us. Besides, if you decide to return, make it during the racing season."

"Sure," replied Flint. "I'll even mark your racing form."

"The last horse I bet on is still running," said Morin.

"We'll pick only winners this time," Flint insisted. "We'll definitely make it for the *Travers Stakes*."

"You have a date," Morin agreed. Then, changing the subject, added, "Look, Flint, this mob thing in Saratoga is nothing new, we all know it. They've changed the rules of the game somewhat, just as I mentioned in Quebec. It's been worked out between the major families and I don't see any trouble brewing, other than the federal people making a move on some of the mob when the timing is right."

"How close are they?" asked Flint.

"That depends on which phase of the Feds' investigation you're talking about. I know some mob people are very nervous over a certain jockey whose name I won't mention here; they might even have him marked."

"Why is that?"

"He's been known to kick a few races in Florida with mounts he should easily have won on. Sources say the Feds think he was involved in a "boat race" involving a champion money-winning three-year-old mare that raced in Saratoga last season...he suddenly became a big spender after the Florida races."

"I heard some talk of this," said Flint. "I mentioned it to Harry, but he seemed surprised."

"Harry's not always in tune with everything," Morin reminded him. "He's too obsessed with the dope thing to get concerned about horses."

"What's the other phase of the investigation?" Flint asked.

"You're back to drugs here," he told Flint. "Horse drugs, that is. You see, they're coming up with new drugs every week. The Federal Government can't keep up with them. They're being shot into the horses before they are officially illegal. The mob is taking advantage of this gap in Federal regulations. Then, of course, street drugs are being used by race employees and jockeys. This is expensive. Expensive habits drive the users to any means to cover their gig. There's a story going round that well-known veterinarians are on the take. It goes on and on. You're familiar with the game, I'm sure."

"Yes, I suppose I am," Flint sighed. "But I hate to see Saratoga tainted so."

"It's pretty bad," admitted Morin. "You'll see

some nasty press coming out on it soon. Once the newspapers start unraveling it all, the Feds will have to move fast. It could be the most interesting summer Saratoga has seen in years."

"Not the type I'm looking for," Flint insisted unhappily. "Thanks for your input. I hope to be up and around within two or three weeks. Get in touch with me then. I'm coming to Saratoga to finish this matter."

"I'll help all I can," said Morin. "One more thing. I contacted Dr. Blake at the hospital. He said he removed the package...he didn't elaborate on the details."

"That's all he said?" asked Flint.

"He said not to be concerned, that everything went smoothly; that was all."

"No complications at all?" Flint asked tensely.

"None whatsoever," answered Morin. "What package was he referring to?"

"A sack of Colombian coffee beans," Flint replied. "It's a private joke -- I'll tell you about it in Saratoga."

"Take care," Morin reminded him. "Don't come East until you feel up to it, promise?"

"I promise," said Flint, closing off the long conversation. Monica returned to the bedroom. "I saw the light go off. That call mustta cost a million."

"Not quite," Flint said. "But It was worth a million!"

She looked at him. "I don't like the tone of your voice," said Monica. "It has a distant ring to it."

"I told you; I have to complete this thing."

"Why don't you get some sleep, Flint. We can discuss it later."

She drew the window shade and went out, shutting the door slowly.

15. Sandy, Sandy, Sandy

Flint spent a restless, boring July in convalescence. Weeks he thought would never end. He'd been good to a degree, not touching one cigarette nor taking any hard liquor all during the recovery period. He was able to move around freely and do some light exercises by late July, but he still wasn't in top shape and he knew it.

He hadn't seen Sandy, though on several occasions he tried to get Monica to take him to see her. Monica turned him down. At times he felt like a hostage in his own home. Monica was almost too protective, he thought, acting like an impenetrable shield between he and Sandy. She tended to his needs willingly and efficiently, coming each morning before heading to her studio, and stopping by each evening to prepare dinner.

Without his permission or knowledge, Monica had hired private bodyguards to watch Flint's cottage during the hours she was absent. And instinctively, after Sandy's arrival in California, she had done the same at her home. It would be poor policy to mention the bodyguards to Flint, she reasoned, his macho pride wouldn't accept it.

He was napping when he heard her car pull up the driveway. He heard the kitchen door slam and the rustle of paper bags being set on the kitchen table. It was nearing six o'clock, almost time for dinner. Monica came into the room, pausing a moment to catch her breath. "The star returns," he declared.

"Naturally," breathed Monica. "A command performance."

"Good," he said. "I'm starved."

"Well, we won't be eating fancy tonight. I picked up a few things from the deli, including some very sour pickles...you like pickles, don't you?"

"You know what I like," he answered. Then, for the first time in months, he remembered how wonderful she could be in bed. "How performance-minded are you?" he asked with one arm outstretched.

She pushed his arm away. "You really are a miserable bastard, Flint, aren't you?"

"I always get romantic when I'm hungry!"

"Then I suggest you eat."

"It can wait," he said.

"No, it can't," she replied. "I'm starved and I'm going to eat. If you care to join me, I'll be on the patio."

Later he joined her outside. She had put together some sliced chicken with pineapple chunks, and had made a tossed salad. The sun was now on the rim of the ocean and it glared orange and red over the rolling surf. Neither spoke throughout the meal. It was almost like the calm before the storm, and Flint knew it.

"I want to see Sandy before I go," he said suddenly without looking up.

"Well," she answered, "you'll probably do whatever you want, won't you?"

"Not exactly."

"Yes, you will."

"Look, Monica," he said, "you did me a favor

by taking her in. You also took care of me all this time and I appreciate that, you know it. If you'd rather I return to Saratoga without seeing Sandy, I'll respect your wish. After all, you've kept her safe and out of harm's way. Maybe I shouldn't try to see her at this time." She remained silent.

"Well," he said again, "shall I go without seeing her, or what?"

"Flint, you know what you must do," she said at length.

"Yes, I guess I do. But I think it's best if you bring her to some other location."

"Hell, no," cried Monica. "Let her stay right at my place. And what's more, let's stop acting like two high school lovers who don't know how to make the break. Christ, we're both well over the hill for that nonsense, aren't we?"

"I suppose we are," he answered. "But I can't congratulate myself for the way things have turned out for you."

"What's the matter, Mike?" she said, smiling at him now. "You becoming sentimental because of me?"

"I care a lot about you."

"Look," she said softly, "let's close this thing by at least keeping our friendship!" She clasped her hands and stood up. "I'll let Sandy know you're coming. Why not make it tonight? I have a dinner date at nine. The timing will be just right."

It was shortly after Flint was again up and around that he discovered that someone was watching his home. He'd seen the car from his side window several times, and noticed that they parked on alternate sides of the road every other night. He always had lived in an atmosphere of self-protectiveness. A simple phone call to a friend in the business in L.A. confirmed that he was being watched over, and that the men had been employed by Monica. In a way, he was pleased that Monica had taken this precaution. He didn't mention it, though, out of respect for her judgment and loyalty.

To avoid upsetting the bodyguards, and alerting anyone else who might be watching his place, he slipped out of the side door, went along a small path near the cliff and out thought his neighbor's drive, coming out well below where their car was parked this evening. He'd made arrangements to meet a private limo in the Palos Verdes Plaza a short distance away, and it was waiting for him when he arrived at the Plaza.

Monica's house was situated closer to L.A., with a clear view of the ocean. Using a side entrance known to few people, Flint avoided the men watching her place and slipped into her living room undetected. One small light was on in the front hallway; the rest of the house was dark except for a light coming from the rear study. He walked quietly into the study at precisely the moment Sandy came out of the kitchen. She looked up, startled, and dropped a glass of iced tea she was carrying. Flint put his finger to his lips and then motioned her toward the living room.

She was swept up in his strong arms, a sob in her throat coming quickly between a series of short kisses. Her body pressed close to his.

Finally she leaned back, trembling with excitement, repeating, "My God, Flint, it's you...it's really you."

He couldn't answer. He kissed her forehead, her cheeks, her lips, her nose. He held her tight against his chest.

"I thought you'd never make it," she found herself saying further. "I had these terrible nightmares shortly after my arrival in California that you would be killed in Quebec. I would wake, night after night, with the same dream. But now you're here...God, you're here!"

"Sandy...Sandy...Sandy," he said in a choking voice.

"I wanted to come and help when they brought you home," she interrupted. "Monica thought it best I stay here."

"I know, my dear, I know, Monica told me. It doesn't matter now."

She pulled him closer. "I felt terribly alone in this huge city," she said. "Monica has been wonderful."

Sandy's hair was combed straight back like a teenager's and caught at the nape of her neck. She raised a tear-stained face to his. He guided her into the living room where it was dark, and quietly they undressed each other and settled on the soft deep carpet between the couch and the fireplace.

"Monica will have a fit," he said softly. "The two of us soiling her carpet!"

"I'll buy her a new one," she whispered, stroking his hair.

She clung to him long after her body had gone limp. She could feel and sense his love seeping into her consciousness and whole being. The fear that it might not last crossed her mind, like the dreams that had been haunting her, so she held him closer.

After a time, with his arms still firmly wrapped around her, he said, "My work in Saratoga isn't finished...you must know that."

She didn't want to hear these words, but she knew he had to say them. She felt hopeless. "Will there ever be an end to this nasty business, Flint?"

"Probably not," he answered simply. "It goes on and on. It always will. Yet I'm very close to cracking this one. I believe I can find Robin's killer if I go back to Saratoga. Do you want me to go back?"

She took his hand and kissed it. "It's something you must do, isn't it?"

"Yes, it's something I must do," he replied. "You know better than anyone that I must complete this investigation. Naturally I have no illusions about the further risks involved."

"I want you to do it for Robin," she said finally. "I also want you to come back to me. Promise me one thing, that you won't go to Quebec again!"

"Quebec is strictly off my list from now on," he laughed.

"Promise," she insisted.

"I promise."

They remained in each other's arms for what seemed an endless evening. They made love again and later, with the lights in the kitchen and study turned down so Flint wouldn't be seen by the bodyguards, she made sandwiches and coffee.

Before he left, he sat with her at the small round study table and stared at her in deep thought. "There's something I must tell you," he said soberly. "Now's as good a time as ever to let this out...at least to let you know."

She shrugged her shoulders, her eyes studying him. "What is it?"

He gnawed at his lower lip. "I was once in love with your mother."

He waited for her startled reaction, but there was none.

"It doesn't come as a shock...as a surprise?" he asked.

"It no doubt will shock Mother," she replied, raising her dark eyebrows. "It won't change a thing between you and me. Mother and I haven't been on the best of terms lately. In fact I haven't seen her in a year. She stays pretty much to herself in Boston. Certainly, if we were on a better one-to-one relationship, she'd be making inquiries as to my sudden disappearance from Saratoga...she's probably not even aware I've left. That will show you how close we are."

Flint sucked in a breath. "That evening at *Lillian's*, I knew," he admitted. "You resemble her so much."

She smiled back, adding, "You're the one she's always carried a torch for. You probably never knew that."

"Oh, no. We ended it without her wanting to see me again."

"Don't let the fact that she married shortly after fool you, Flint. She always was in love with you."

"That was a long time ago," he added.

"Women have long memories," she insisted. "Mother had a miserable marriage. Actually she's never been too settled...my father died about five years ago and she's been living like a semi-recluse ever since. She's well-off but she doesn't know how to live. It's the reason I got out on my own just as soon as I could. It wasn't so much a point of being independent, but I knew if I stayed at home, some of her negativism might rub off...it's the truth, so why hide it!"

"I didn't want to return to Saratoga without telling you about my involvement with your mother," he said in a gentle voice.

"I'm glad you did," she murmured.

Her eyes met his again, and she moved over to kiss him. He was relieved that she had accepted this revelation, though he had doubts her mother ever would if, at any time in the future, she became aware of it.

They spent another hour together, then Flint knew he must finally leave.

"I don't want you to go, even though I know

you must," she said in a depressed tone.

"I'll be back, my darling...I'll be back. That you can count on!"

She cried when he left.

Monica didn't return until morning. She found Sandy asleep on the divan in the study. She didn't disturb her. Later in the day, however, they had something to eat and they discussed Flint's decision to return to Saratoga. It was a decision both knew they had no chance of changing.

Flint flew out of L.A. International Airport the next morning, August third. Saratoga's race season was opening the next day.

16. He's My Main Man

F lint did not use the mansion on this trip to Saratoga. Instead he rented a room on the outskirts of town on Route 9. It was the only accommodation he could find because Saratoga was now filled with summer tourists. He passed himself off as a fellow from New York City, spending the month of August going to the track. He used the Saratoga taxis for transportation, noting that they were numerous and readily available most of the time, day or night.

On his third day back he decided it was time he found out about Marty Dresser. He thumbed through the phone directory, but couldn't find her listed. He called information, and they had no listing either.

He made some inquiries in town, but still could not come up with her number or a solid address. He moved about in Saratoga with more caution than he had on his previous stay, making certain that he wasn't being tailed. At night, wearing different disguises, he made frequent rounds to some of the sleazy haunts, in hopes of picking up information on Marty.

The local cops would know exactly where her place was located, but there was no way he could approach them. Then, one evening he noticed an unescorted girl sitting at a bar on the west side of town. She looked like a college type who was very drunk -- or drugged -- and strictly out of her class in this joint. He moved in beside her and ordered a drink. She looked up with round, red-rimmed eyes and blinked. "Buy me a drink...drink," she insisted, slobbering her words.

"How about a coke?"

"The hell with that...I want a drink...a real drink."

"OK, what'll it be?"

"Vodka...straight up on the glass...I mean rocks...rocks."

"I don't think we've met," Flint said.

"We haven't," she snapped back.

"I'm Tom Black," he said.

"Helen...Helen Wallingsford."

"Would you care to sit at a table, Helen?" Flint offered.

"Why not?" she replied.

He ordered her drink and watched as she quickly sipped it down, making her even more tipsy. She had rust-colored hair, tied back tightly, and wore a bedraggled flowery-print summer dress. Her eyes were pale blue, with dark circles beneath them. She apparently had been on something heavy earlier in the day, and the vodka was being used to stand off a crash until she could get some more of whatever-it-was.

"Do you know who I am?" she asked suddenly, looking at him as if he should know. "You may not think it, but I'm quite young and I have respectability -- I come from money. Do you believe that?"

"Yeah, I can believe that," Flint agreed.

"These creeps in here know that...you bet they know that," she said, waving her arms and pointing. "They should know, Goddammit, "I've pissed a lot of my money away in here...."

"Why do you swear so much?" he asked.

174

"I don't swear too much," she insisted.

"Maybe you don't know you swear so much," he warned her.

"Actually I don't like swearing...I'll try not to swear anymore, OK?"

"Fine by me."

The room was very dark and almost empty. One couple remained at the bar and a few strays sat at tables at the far end near the rear exit. It was Thursday night, and Flint wondered why there wasn't more activity.

"Why is it so dead?" he asked.

"They're at the party, silly...they'll be back later."

"Oh, I forgot," he said, picking up on her cue. "I completely forgot."

"Marty won't like that," she said with a wide smile. "She'll take you off her guest list, Tommy old-boy."

He leaned forward when she said the name, his ears straining to catch it again.

"I really forgot where her place is," he baited her.

"Nonsense," she spit the word out. "It's not that hard to find."

"Then let's go," he said lightheartedly.

"Nah," she mumbled. "Marty's got me on her shit list already."

Flint was becoming anxious. "Come on, you can go as my guest." "Nah...forget it. I'll wait till they come back."

He slid his chair around next to her and whispered, "I tell you what. You come with me and I'll give you some little pills that will blow your mind. You can stay in the car if you like...I'll go to the party for a little bit, and then we'll come back together...what do ya say?"

He noticed her hands moving frantically around her glass. He desperately wanted to get her out of the bar before she became too far gone and started having hallucinations. He hoped she'd remember how to get to Marty's place.

"I got no money...nothing. I'm broke," she said, her voice trailing off.

"This one's on me," he encouraged her. "Now let's go. Come on, before it's over!"

She nodded her approval, and they went outside. They walked away from the bar toward town. She glanced up and asked, "Where's your car?"

"We'll catch a cab," he said. "I'm too drunk to drive."

"Be my leader...be my leader," she called out.

Flint stopped at a pay booth and called Saratoga Taxi. "I need a cab fast, can you come right away?" he asked, identifying himself as Tom Black.

"It'll be there in three minutes," the dispatcher said. "Where to?"

"The other side of town," Flint said. "Yaddo Park."

"Right away, hang on."

He practically had to lift her into the cab when it arrived. She was both drunk and tired. He held her upright once inside and rubbed the back of her neck to keep her from falling asleep. In a barrage of broken sentences, she directed the driver past the racetrack, down a long dirt road, around the back of the Yaddo and down yet two more twisting dirt roads. "It's further down...down...keep going," Helen babbled.

Flint was beginning to doubt her. "Are you sure?" he asked.

"We're all right, Tommy boy. I know the way."

The cab driver turned his head. "This looks like a dead end."

"No...no...no," she insisted. "We have to make another turn."

"Where are we?" asked Flint.

"We're almost there," she cried angrily. "Why don't you believe me!"

She began crying uncontrollably.

"It's OK," Flint said. "Stop crying! We believe you."

Then just ahead they saw faint lights. Flint estimated they were about two hundred yards away. The driver suddenly spun the wheel and turned into another dirt road which actually was a long driveway.

Flint turned to Helen. "I guess you were right."

She began to mutter something, then giggled and fell over on the rear seat, out cold. Her face was pushed against the back of the seat and Flint had to turn it away to keep her from suffocating.

"Is she OK?" the driver asked.

"She'll be fine," Flint answered. "Let her sleep it off. Don't go any further. I'll get out here. Trn around, shut off your lights and wait for me. I shouldn't be too long."

"I'll drive you to the door," the cabby insisted.

"No," Flint said in a dry, hurried voice. "I want to surprise them. Do you have a flashlight?"

"Yeah, there's one here someplace."

He found the light under the seat and handed it to Flint. Flint flashed it on Helen's face before getting out of the cab. She was breathing heavily, open-mouthed.

"Keep a close watch on her. I'll be back shortly," he said, and left.

He counted a dozen cars and vans parkcd near the cottage. Music was coming from within as he approached the front door, a very low guitar solo. He didn't hear any voices. The door was partly open. He pushed, and it swung completely open. The strong smell of body odor hit him. He retreated a step to get away from it, but then continued inside. Bodies were strewn about the huge room. Some on the floor, some on couches and lounge chairs, and two or three huddled near the fireplace which wasn't burning.

Then he realized he had stumbled into a bizarre community drug pad.

He figured they had been at it for hours. They were all bombed out. Flint hurried through some of the other rooms, holding his hand to his nose to keep from getting sick from the odor. He went upstairs and checked out the bedrooms. Several more were draped over the beds, and he found one girl, not much more than eighteen, passed out on the bathroom floor.

He went back downstairs, stepping over a body or two, to get to the door for a breath of air. A momentary breeze gave him some relief from the smell.

"Hello, stranger," a soft voice called out.

Flint turned back to the room. He didn't see anyone.

"Say hello to Marty!"

Then he saw the strange round face, smiling up at him from the couch. It was wet with perspiration and puffy like a jellyfish. He moved slowly toward her. She had on a dirty red robe that was open between her breasts. She was as thin as a rail, Flint noted, with mousy brown hair on a head much too large for her body. Her legs were tucked up under the robe and one bony foot was visible. He could tell that she once had a pretty face, and her hazel eyes still had the gleam of intelligence. He couldn't help but feel pity for the emaciated girl in front of him.

"I guess I'm late for this party," he said. "I don't want to disturb anyone."

"You're not disturbing anyone," she assured him.

"Then it's all right if I stay awhile?"

"Sit down, man. Enjoy...enjoy!"

He took a step closer to her, then decided to

sit in a chair a few feet away, for he wasn't sure he could get through the conversation without vomiting.

"Do I know you?" she asked.

"In a vague sort of way," he replied.

"That's funny," she continued. "I can't place you."

"I'm a friend of Helen's...Helen Wallingsford," he felt uneasy while saying it.

Her eyes met his. They opened and shut like a sucker's mouth, and the dull glaze remained in them. Flint took out a cigarette and lit it, while trying to show no sign of distaste, especially for the vile heap of bodies surrounding him.

"Hey, baby, get yourself a real smoke," she said. She stretched out her hand and he saw it held some reefers. "Go on, honey, smoke one of these," she offered, with her eyes still blinking. Then she leaned back and gazed at him defiantly.

He hadn't smoked pot in years, but he took it anyway. She watched as he lit it and drew in a long drag, letting it out slowly and partly through his nose. He would do anything at this point to keep from arousing her suspicion and hold her attention. She looked as if she was on the verge of crashing also.

"Oh, Marty," he breathed. "You got the real stuff all right...this is fine...fine...fine!"

"My Main Man says it's the best in the East."

"Your Main Man? Who's that?"

"He ain't got no name...but he's my Main Man. He comes up with the best of everything. You should've been here when this party started. Why, we began with reefers, and moved into the real sauce fast. This conclave won't come out of it till morning...they've had the course, wouldn't you say?"

He nodded and took another drag. "You have real staying power, Marty. What's your secret?"

"I get more practice than the rest," she laughed, and her cheeks turned red, the skin just above the chin set in wrinkles. It looked like a worn-out oilcloth.

"My Main Man treats me right," she repeated. "Do you know something? He'll be here for the races next week."

"He's a horse buff?" asked Flint, waiting for a reaction from her.

"Hell, no. He wouldn't go near a horse."

"But he likes racing."

"Wrong again," she teased him.

"You got me stumped," Flint admitted. "You'll just have to tell me."

She didn't answer. Instead she popped a small white pill into her mouth and Flint watched as she gulped it down dry, her face a pathetic mask. He waited for a time before going on. He was certain she would break down before long.

Her right hand raised suddenly and clapped over her mouth. She held her abdomen with her left hand. He knew she was in pain. She showed all the symptoms of a person reaching overdose. The redness left her cheeks and her face turned ashen.

"Christ," he whispered aloud. "She's going to die right in front of me."

She sat there for several moments in this condition, and suddenly it was gone. Flint was amazed. She raised her head and began talking as if nothing had happened.

"Oh, yes, you still don't know who my Main Man is?"

"You tell me," he said.

"I told you, dummy, he doesn't have a name."

Flint tried another approach. "It doesn't matter, Marty. If that's the way it is, that's the way it is. Let's forget him. Let's talk about you."

Her eyes lit up and he knew she was delighted

180

with this suggestion.

"Sure, why not?" she agreed.

"You throw the best parties, right? You know the best people, right? You got money, right?" he prodded her along. "You're bright, right? You went to school at Skidmore, right?"

"Stop it...stop it," she cried. "Don't mention Skidmore to me!"

"Oh, sorry," said Flint. "I didn't know it would bother you."

"I got kicked out...you must know that. Everyone else does."

"I guess I forgot. The hell with it, it's a dump anyway, right?"

"Right," she repeated.

He was about to go on when suddenly her eyes watered, and she fell to one side on the couch clutching her abdomen once again.

"Balls...balls," she cried out. "What the hell did he give me?"

"Who's he?" screamed Flint.

"Georgio...Georgio...that rat fink!"

Flint sat dumbfounded. He became oblivious to Marty's apparent suffering. His mind turned inward. He didn't even notice that she was foaming at the mouth. A slow anger overcame him as he digested the name. Yes, Georgio, why hadn't he figured it out earlier? Even when Morin suggested it in Quebec, he had brushed it back. Who else could have known? Who else could have set him up? It was Georgio all along.

That's what St. Jacques was trying to tell him. It must have been Georgio who tipped St. Jacques off about his Quebec visit. All of the past few months suddenly flashed through his mind....*Yes*. And the connection with the little frightened white ghost of a girl foaming at the mouth in front of him now all made sense. Georgio was after her land. Hell, he had a virtual death grip on her by keeping her drugged.

He snapped back to the present when he heard her belch. She did so several times before getting sick all over the couch. Flint waited to see that she would come out if it alive. After a while she stopped vomiting; however, she was too ill to talk further.

He eased his way out of the house and hurried back to the waiting cab. Helen was still sleeping. He lifted her into a sitting position and got in beside her.

"I didn't think you were coming back," said the driver.

"Sorry I stayed so long," said Flint. "They didn't want me to leave."

"What's going on in there, anyway?" the driver asked.

"They're having a going-away party," Flint answered. "It's their last fling."

Back in town they woke Helen and left her a short distance from the bar where Flint had met her. Flint shoved twenty dollars into her dress before leaving her. As the cab moved away, Flint watched her walk slowly toward the bar with a staggering gait.

Flint got off on mid-Broadway. He went into a small lounge near Caroline Street and had a drink. He needed time now to reason out his next move.

17. After All These Years

A fresh summer breeze blew through Flint's window the next morning, waking him from a sound sleep. He cursed himself for having had one too many drinks because his head hurt. In his mind he retraced his steps again and again. His thought processes were working overtime long before he stepped into the shower and had dressed for the day.

He heard a car motor down in the street, and going to the window he observed two men getting into a black sedan. They were track hands staying at the same rooming house. It wasn't quite six-thirty, but he knew their day started early -- especially this day, for it was the beginning of the *Fasig-Tipton Yearling Sales.*

Flint had to decide exactly how to approach Central concerning Georgio. Tipping Harry off would accomplish nothing, he reasoned. Harry would probably strangle the bastard on the spot. Any communication with Central might alert Georgio also. He had the feeling that Georgio would be in Saratoga for the sales, if for no other reason than to peddle drugs, because the money was flowing freely at this time. And there was always the possibility that Marty had already contacted Georgio after Flint's visit last night. His only hope on this score was that Marty wouldn't recall what he looked like, which would leave Georgio to speculate who it was she did talk to.

If Georgio was coming to Saratoga, he no doubt would be at the sales, or at least the track. Marty's naive assumption that Georgio did not like horses amused Flint, for he knew Georgio to be addicted to the ponies.

The little town was crowding up with track goers, but Flint felt confident that he could locate Georgio. Whether he could isolate him, once found, would be another problem.

Flint had several priority items on his agenda, one of which was contacting Dr. Blake. He left the rooming house and walked down Broadway to use a pay phone on the corner near the Firehouse Restaurant. Dr. Blake was surprised when Flint said hello in his usual casual tone.

"You really are alive," said Blake, trying to sound relaxed. "I've got nine lives, didn't you know that, Doc?"

"How is Sandy?" asked Blake.

"Fine...fine," replied Flint. "She's still in L.A. She's safer there, I think you'll agree?"

"Yes, I suppose you're right. We had some time explaining her sudden departure from Saratoga. The doctors and nurses still look at me with a jaundiced eye when her name comes up in conversation around the hospital."

"That's to be expected," agreed Flint.

"It makes me nervous," admitted Blake. "I talk to liars all day, but I'm not used to being one."

"In this case, you're justified," said Flint.

"Let's hope so," Blake replied.

Flint continued, "I gather from the police reports that our other matter was settled without anyone the wiser?"

"Yes," said Blake. "As I told your associate Morin, we moved the bod...I mean the package and it was done without incident."

"I'm dying to know how," added Flint.

"I did it with Benson's help. I needed a strong back at the time."

"Pardon me for asking," said Flint, "but where in hell did you put it?"

"Oh, didn't you hear?" Dr. Blake mused. "It showed up in New York City as just another gang war victim. Case closed. And don't talk about it anymore or I'll get a compulsion to go to confession over it."

"Thanks, Doc. Look, I know who's behind this. He's probably in Saratoga right now. I also paid a visit to Marty...remember, the one mentioned in Robin's note. She's a pothead living near Yaddo. The guy I'm after is trying to rip off her land, at least the land now owned by her grandparents that will soon be hers. I can't go into it all now, but if things go right, I'll have this in the bag by the end of the week. Sit tight and I'll let you know how I make out."

"If I can be of any further help, just call," Blake offered.

"I just may need some help," said Flint.

"Watch yourself," warned Blake.

"I'll do that, Doc. Take care."

After he hung up, he placed a long distance call to Morin in Montreal. It was the only way he could think of to make contact with Central without letting anyone know his real location. In fact, he reasoned, it might even throw Georgio off track. It would suit his purpose better if he could make Georgio think he was in Canada.

Flint decided he would let Morin use his code to call Central. Under normal operating procedures Flint was sworn to secrecy concerning his special code. Hell, he thought, this is not a normal situation. He went over the details with Morin when the call was finally put through.

Morin was shocked when he learned that it was Georgio, even though he'd considered that possibility and, like Flint, rejected it. "After all these years..." he said.

"I guess we can expect anything in this game," Flint said. "I shouldn't have dismissed it so quickly."

"If you want me to come down, I will," Morin offered. "I'll bring LaDuke if you want him."

"No. I can handle Georgio, now that I know the score, but thanks anyway."

"It's always safer to have some back-up," Morin insisted.

"If it gets too heavy, I'll call you," Flint said. "By the way, when this is all over I'm going to buy you and LaDuke the finest meal I can find...I'll even throw in a bottle of vintage wine."

"I'll take you up on that," agreed Morin, then adding, "tread easy, Flint. Georgio is no fool. He carries a lot of clout. I see now why St. Jacques wanted to have you take care of him. He's probably got enough information to blow the entire lid off the mob connection. In short, they can't touch him...you can. Don't give him too much rope!"

"Thanks for the advice, and for everything you did," said Flint. "I'll play this close to the vest."

"I'm here if you need me, remember."

"You'll be hearing from me," said Flint.

He had breakfast on the patio of the *Firehouse Restaurant.* The early morning sun blazed down on Saratoga, and already the main street was busy with cars going by and people out walking. Flint found it hard to believe that so much intrigue could be associated with this small city. Certainly it was far from the thoughts and cares of the tourists parading about Saratoga.

He decided that he would begin looking for Georgio at the *Yearling Sales* that evening.

18. Going Once, Going Twice...

I t was one of those uniquely beautiful August evenings in Saratoga. As Flint approached the pavilion at the start of the *Yearling Sales*, he turned his eyes upward to the sky and observed a million twinkling specks. A gentle night breeze swept through the area, taking away the last of the day's humidity. The crowd was already gathering. He watched in quiet amazement the long line of limousines inching toward the pavilion's main entrance as the buyers rushed to get inside before the auctioneer's hammer officially opened the evening's sale.

These were the real money people, the tycoons of big business, the family bloodlines that had amassed fortunes over the years. A duke or a princess might mingle here and there among the new and old rich of America and Europe.

"Oh, yes," someone in the crowd outside was heard to say, "there goes Mrs. Willis. Her husband owns a hundred oil wells. She's heiress to millions on her father's side also."

Saratoga was drawing them all. A well-known movie star could be spotted within the pavilion, leaning over to talk to friends.

Flint could see the glitter of diamonds sparkling in the pavilion's well-lit interior. Some of the women wore long gowns, others were in smartly tailored pantsuits. Men were in suits with narrow pinstripes for the most part, but many wore dark blazers and slacks. An occasional light gold or plaid blazer could be seen, generally worn by the younger men.

The *Yearling Sales* represented the highlight of the season for many of the crowd here tonight. Some would remain for the whole month of racing, but others were in town for the sales alone and would be leaving after making their purchases. Four nights of thoroughbred auctions, bringing together the finest young horseflesh in the world.

Flint noticed a group of fifteen or more people marching just a short distance from the pavilion. They were protesting against the millions being spent on horses while men, women and children in the world were starving to death. Some of their placards read *"Tax Breaks for the Rich and Horses, While the World Goes Hungry."*

Flint moved around slowly. He went out to the back of the pavilion to the walking ring where already two yearlings were waiting to be taken inside for the first showing of the evening. Several buyers, trainers and jockeys were waiting near the ring, discussing last bits and pieces of information on the pedigree of specific colts and fillies. Rumor was floating around the sales that the average price for a yearling would be $180,000, and some horses were expected to bid out at over a million. The name of the game was to get a yearling with good potential at a steal; especially one from a leading American sire or stakes winner. The knowledgeable old-timers would be going against the new buyers, and the competitive spirit during the sales had increased the price of the yearlings dramatically in the past five years, Flint had learned.

There was no doubt about it. These monied

people lived in a very different world from the average wage earner. And in spite of all the money, in spite of the protesters, in spite of the public's loss of faith in the integrity of horse racing of late, the game goes on, Flint mused. He reasoned that the sport was bigger than all of them.

Further on he stopped at the sales building and picked up a copy of the sales book for the evening. He obtained a copy of the sire reference update and breeder's index.

A couple of neatly dressed fillies of the two-legged variety brushed by him, and he gave them a well-deserved glance. Another clung to her father's arm and remarked, "Will you really buy that one for me, Daddy?"

Television monitors were located at various points on the sales grounds so viewers could keep track of the bidding on each thoroughbred. Flint turned to look at one just as the sale began.

"Now ladies and gentlemen, before we begin the sale this evening, I must remind everyone wishing to make a purchase that unless credit has already been established with *Fasig-Tipton Company, Inc.*, or its subsidiary, any purchases here tonight will be for cash only. We'll take good old American dollars or certified checks. Thank you. Now let's get on with the sale."

The first yearling of the sale was led onto the green synthetic carpet in front of the auctioneer's stand, and the tempo inside the pavilion picked up as the bidding began.

"Now here's a fine bay colt by a winner of six stakes races, a half brother to *Benjie's Joy*, sired by *Run for the Money* and the dam, *Catcher If You Can*. Do I hear an opening bid of $60,000 for this colt?"

The auctioneer's voice boomed over the PA system. One of the spotters motioned an opening bid and the auctioneer continued. "Surely this animal is worth more than the opening bid. You might be sorry tomorrow you didn't take a better look at this opportunity...do I hear sixty-five?"

The extra sales pitch drew another five grand. That jumped quickly to seventy thousand, then eighty, then ninety. "Going once, going twice. Gone for ninety thousand!" said the auctioneer. "Good luck, and thank you, John," he added, acknowledging the buyer whom he recognized immediately.

The next horse was quickly brought into the pavilion and pranced around by a groom, and the bidding proceeded.

Flint watched a dozen or so horses enter the pavilion, and noticed that two particular buying groups seated directly in front of the auctioneer were dominating the early bidding. He then moved to the front of the structure so he could see through the large plate glass windows. It was a spectacle for anyone to watch.

His eyes roamed carefully over the crowd inside. He followed each row of seats, first downstairs and then in the gallery. He knew there were front men for the mob seated somewhere inside, though he couldn't identify any of them. They would be doing the buying for the bosses who couldn't get near this particular gathering. In this extremely fast battle of wits, with thousands going down every four or five minutes, Flint knew that dollars that had been milked from the Helens and Martys of this world would be buying some mobster a racehorse or two. He really wasn't interested in their involvement except that indirectly they were probably as responsible for Robin's death as Georgio was. It stemmed from their trafficking in drugs. The slimy streams eventually filled one big cesspool one had to detest.

Over a hundred horses were scheduled to be auctioned, which meant that the sales would last until some time after 10 p.m. Flint checked his watch; they still had an hour to go. He was tempted to leave the sales and check out Marty's place once more. If Marty hadn't contacted Georgio, there was always the possibility he could get additional information as to Georgio's real plans. On second thought he dismissed this impulse. Georgio's passion for horses would lead him to the sales. Unless, of course, he wasn't in town yet.

The game Flint was now playing was similar to the counter-intelligence work he had done while in the C.I.A. Go with your hunches. Be steadfast. Try to figure the other guy's next move. Make the flow come your way. It all seemed very rudimentary, yet it didn't always work.

There was a sudden excitement among the crowd. Flint turned and looked at the monitor to his left. A chestnut colt by a leading Irish stakes winner was being purchased for one million, two hundred thousand. The crowd both inside and outside the pavilion let out a cheer as the auctioneer's hammer fell on the sale to a buyer from Southern California.

The camera followed the horse out of the pavilion where another portable camera picked up the action. Everyone was gaping and talking as the stallion passed by the ring and was led to the barn area. Flint watched the graceful stride of the horse and the careful handling by the grooms, now all aware they were touching a million dollar piece of property. One man with a flash camera ran up and wanted to take a shot. He was pushed aside by a guard who said, "We don't allow pictures here."

"C'mon," the man insisted. "I just want one."

The guard put up his hand. "No pictures!"

He gave the guard a dejected look, put the camera back in its case and left.

Another colt, predicted earlier as a possible big-money horse, entered the pavilion. There was a scramble for positions in front of all the outside monitors as the bidding began.

Flint directed his attention to the monitor once more.

Between bids the camera quickly swept back and forth across the pavilion's interior, identifying some of the more prominent stable owners. As it crossed the gallery and dropped to the section just to the right of the stairs, Flint's heart jumped a pace. He leaned forward and took another look.

Seated in the third row of the lower balcony he spotted Georgio. The smug mustached face was turned slightly, and he was talking to a slim woman with dark hair. The camera moved on to another section of the pavilion.

Flint went as fast as he could to the building's front and took up a position near the entrance. There were too many obstacles in his path, and too many spectators, so he moved to the left of the building which gave him a clearer view of the balcony. He could feel the anger building within himself. He kept his eyes fixed on the balcony. Not for one second did he want to lose sight of Georgio.

He waited nervously for over a half hour as the bidding continued, watching Georgio make small talk to his elegantly dressed lady friend. He had to fight back the temptation to go right in and wring his neck in front of the million dollar gathering. During the wait, he noticed that Georgio had a male acquaintance as well. A medium built, darkly handsome man in his mid forties or so. Flint figured he was no doubt tied to drugs.

The last of the horses were led into the pavilion and the hammer fell at last on the final sale of the evening. Flint watched Georgio and his companions stand up and move toward the stairs. He went to the main entrance door again and, huddled near one of the pillars, he waited for them to make their exit. They came out surrounded by several buyers and Flint at one point could have reached out and touched Georgio if he had so desired.

Cars were pulling up to the entrance whisking the crowd away, and Flint overheard Georgio's male friend tell the driver of their car to head for the *Gideon Putnam Hotel* in the Spa Park. The car door slammed and they were gone. Flint glared as it sped away and he saw Georgio's face beaming with a smile, one arm around his lady friend's shoulders. He also made a mental note of the New York (State) license plate.

Well, Flint thought, the cop goes in style. Not many cops he knew could afford a $150-a-night hotel. He waited for the crowd to thin down. Then he went over to the primrose garden of the nearby *Spuyten Duyvil* and ordered a tall Scotch and water. He decided that things were going to get even more hectic from this point on, so he might just as well enjoy one pleasant evening in Saratoga. He stayed at the *Duyvil* the remainder of the night, watching the beautiful and the rich mingle. His only regret was that he couldn't share it with Sandy.

19. An Elephant On Quicksand

In the morning, with his head throbbing somewhat, Flint called Central to check on the license plate owner. He purposely avoided contacting Harry on this call. Central's operations officer identified the plate as one registered to Lawrence Smith of West 64th Street in the City. It was a black Cadillac limousine. Flint recalled it was the same car he saw leave the pavilion.

Flint then called the *Gideon Putnam Hotel* to see if either Georgio or Smith was registered. Only Smith's name was on the register. Flint figured Smith was probably a phony name, even though the car was properly registered. They were staying in Suite 123, undoubtedly together, Flint reasoned further. Their good-looking brunette friend of the night before might or might not be staying with them. Georgio trusted few people and had been known in Central over the years as having a contemptuous attitude toward female co-workers. It was unlikely that Georgio would take any woman into his confidence with the stakes so high.

Flint was working with very little evidence, and he knew it. The trick now was to lure Georgio into making a move that would both reveal his real intentions and implicate him with Marty

Dresser. He felt like an elephant tiptoeing over quicksand, aware of the danger but not exactly certain how to approach it. It was now a subtle game and it had to be played right.

It was a safe guess that Marty had not spoken to Georgio, for he looked too relaxed at the sales. Flint had two avenues of approach, he figured. Get Georgio on a one-to-one basis and beat a confession out of him that could be recorded on tape, or surprise him in the act of making a drop either to Marty or someone else. Preferably recorded by camera.

Georgio would worm out of this if Flint didn't come up with some hard evidence, though.

By mid-morning he had made a decision to check out the *Gideon Putnam Hotel*. He had to know Georgio's moves in advance if he were to set anything up. He also would need some help; at least some help with surveillance. Someone would have to watch Marty's place while Flint covered the *Gideon*. He immediately thought of Dr. Blake.

He called Blake on his private line at the hospital. "Didn't think I'd be calling you back so soon," said Flint. "I need some help for a day or two. Can you assist me?"

"I'm on duty for the next three days," replied Dr. Blake, "but I'm sure we can arrange something. What has to be done?"

"I need a good bird watcher," Flint continued. "Someone who can spot a black hawk who wears a dark hat a mile away."

"Sounds like a strange bird," Blake kidded.

"He's really a vulture," Flint said. "But we're soon going to clip his wings and feed them to him for dinner."

Blake thought it over for a moment, then said, "Benson is off. He'll do it if I ask him."

"Do you think he's up to it?" asked Flint.

"He's got more smarts than people give him credit for."

"Fine by me," agreed Flint. "He'll have to watch Marty's place down near Yaddo. It's difficult as hell to find; however, a few drivers at Saratoga Taxi are familiar with the place. Benson will have to be instructed to keep well out of sight. I'm interested only if he spots a black Cadillac approaching the place."

"Sounds like you're finally near to wrapping this mess up?" Blake remarked.

"Could be," said Flint. "It may even be the guy who hired Robin's killer. He's also involved in some very nasty drug dealings and other dirty pool."

"Well, get the son-of-a-bitch for all of us," Blake yelled over the phone. "I'll work this watch thing out with Benson. We have two-way radios here at the hospital that the guards use. I can keep in touch with him easily."

"You should have been a cop," Flint commented.

"When do you want him there?" asked Blake.

"Any time after noon, I guess. The guy I'm looking for should be heading to the races, but we never know. Thanks again, Doc. I'll be in touch. I'll call your number on the half hour. If you're not there, I'll leave a message with Davis... Take care."

"Get the S.O.B.," Blake repeated.

"I intend to, Doc. I intend to."

Flint arrived at the *Gideon Putnam Hotel* just as the brunch crowd was assembling. They were so numerous there was an overflow from the main dining room. Waiters were busy setting up small tables on the patio and porch areas to help accommodate the over-capacity crowd.

Inside at the small service bar the bartender was mixing batch after batch of tall Bloody Marys.

The drinks were being consumed faster than he could mix them. Flint watched the men and women appearing from their rooms. There had been a lot of late-night parties, and he noticed the heavy eyelids and not-yet-awake faces on many of the guests.

It was a hot morning. The hotel's high ceilings had fans circulating the air, but they couldn't cool down the interior because the doors were constantly being opened and closed, letting in the warm, humid air.

Flint went out to the patio and seated himself at a small corner table. He could see the main entrance from this location. He ordered coffee and a hard roll. Earlier he had purchased a newspaper, and he now held it up in front of him, pretending to read.

He also was wearing a disguise. This time he wore a beard which was grey, and he had touched up his sideburns to match. He wore a straw hat, was dressed in a conservative light blue suit, and carried a walnut cane. It made him appear in his mid-sixties. He tipped the newspaper slightly so that his eyes could barely peek over the top to see the entrance. He'd finished two coffees, taking over a half hour to do so, and still there was no sign of Georgio or his friends. The waiter came by several times. Flint knew they were anxious to seat others at his table. The more turnover, the more tips. Eventually he let them have the table.

He walked around the front grounds, still within sight of the entrance. Another thirty minutes slipped by. Then he had an idea. He went inside and found one of the porters. Placing a ten-dollar bill in the porter's palm, he asked him to make a check on the guests in Suite 123. The porter went to the suite and came back within five minutes, reporting that the people in Suite

123 had already checked out for the day, leaving their key at the main desk.

The humidity inside the hotel was getting worse. Perspiration stood out on Flint's temples and he could feel the hot wetness beneath his beard. Then he thought of the room key.

"Do you have an extra key to Suite 123?" he asked the porter quietly.

"No. We don't carry extra keys, sir. Only the manager and the desk clerk can handle keys."

Flint reached in his pocket and took out a hundred-dollar bill. He saw the porter cautiously eye the money.

Flint glanced at the porter. "I need to get in there for a few minutes. Do you understand?"

"The rules are pretty stiff here," the porter replied thoughtfully.

"I can understand that," said Flint. "But rules can be broken, can't they?"

The porter gave him a meaningful look. "It will have to be quick!"

"You let me in. Keep a close watch while I'm in there and when I come out, I'll make that another hundred. Agreed?"

"I'll take the first hundred now," said the porter. Flint nodded and slipped him the bill.

Flint then walked slowly among the hotel guests toward Suite 123. He waited until the porter, using the utmost caution, unlocked the door and, moving swiftly, Flint went inside.

He hurried across the room and began looking through the dresser. He found only a few men's shirts, underwear and socks. The room had two single beds. There was a connecting room which had large French windows. The curtains were open, so he stayed close to the inner walls. He found only men's clothing in the closets, also. It appeared that Georgio and Smith were sharing the suite.

He went back into the bedroom. It was evident to him that Georgio and Smith were traveling light, for there wasn't enough clothing to last for a week's stay. He peered around further. The beds hadn't been made up yet. Flint checked out the nightstands, but found only a pack of cigarettes. Then his foot suddenly kicked something hard under the edge of the bed. He felt under and pulled out a small suitcase. It was unlocked. It contained clothing, also. Flint rolled back some of the garments and a small envelope appeared. He opened it and began looking over its contents.

One piece of paper had a long list of numbers. At first he thought they were telephone numbers, but on further inspection he noticed they only had six digits. His eyes were drawn to the very last page. Written in small, very difficult-to-read handwriting, he noticed Marty's name. There was a series of notes referring to Marty's Saratoga property. One indicated that Lawrence Smith should be given power of attorney in the event of Marty's grandparents' deaths. Another listed a safe deposit box number where the deed to the property was kept. Georgio had done his homework well, Flint thought. He even stayed at arm's length by bringing Smith into the picture. It would all be a very simple transaction. Marty, pickled in the brain, would quietly sign over the property to them when her grandparents no longer existed.

Flint took the page closer to the window light, and slipping a small black cylinder from his inner pocket, he quickly snapped a half-dozen pictures with a special miniature camera, issued by Central, that could self-develop when exposed to light. He then put everything back in its place and slid the case back under the bed as he had found it.

He then noticed another piece of paper on the bed. He hadn't seen it at first because it blended with the white bedspread. It was hastily scribbled in pencil, perhaps taken over the telephone. It read: *"Use the numbers as listed in the ninth race...only the ninth race."*

That was it, he thought, the numbers were a fix. Six digits each. Georgio had been given some inside information on a fix at the track during the ninth race. Perhaps it was a payoff...or a buy-off. But what did they represent? Flint surmised that they were probably triple numbers, or combinations of possible triple numbers.

He opened the suitcase and took some more pictures of the sequence of numbers. When he was finished, he edged toward the door and left the suite. The porter was waiting nearby in the hallway. Flint gave him another hundred dollar bill and departed from the *Gideon Putnam*. The famous *Whitney Stakes* was being run this day at Saratoga as the eighth race. It seemed incredible that the mob would tamper with Saratoga on a Saturday. But who, if anyone, would expect that during the ninth race, a fixed race had been planned, especially a triple?

It would be an interesting day at the Queen of Tracks, Flint thought, as he hailed a cab from the *Gideon*.

"Perhaps I can alter the bastard's plans," he whispered to himself on entering the cab.

"Did you say something?" the driver asked.

"Oh! No," said Flint. "Just take me to the clubhouse entrance."

20. The Party's Over

The horse-crazy crowd was streaming through the gates of the main clubhouse entrance when Flint arrived at the track. After purchasing his ticket, he went out to the paddock to watch the horses for the first race being saddled and readied by their trainers and owners. It was a typically hot, humid Saturday afternoon in August and all the famed racing fraternity seemed to be on hand. Pretty girls with handsome escorts, their mothers and fathers in fashionable race-track attire, and the jockeys, cocky and positive as they mounted the lean, temperamental thoroughbreds.

Flint had always enjoyed the backstretch scene and Saratoga was the perfect place to see it -- more relaxed and accessible. He left the paddock and worked his way back to the clubhouse, pausing for a moment at the turnstile to have his hand stamped, and then continuing through the lower section to come out to the dining area facing the track. Every table was filled. He noticed a man trying to give the table captain a twenty dollar bill to obtain a table. The captain, a short man with an egg-shaped head, smiled politely but shook this head, no. These tables had long since been reserved. Flint knew that occasionally cancellations occurred, but no table captain was going to give one up for twenty dollars, at least not on *Whitney* Saturday.

The table captains are the undisputed masters in the clubhouse, and they get the maximum results during the five week race meet. The smart patrons are willing to slip a hundred or more for a table, and the captains always know who these people are.

The horses were now on the track for the first race and Flint listened as the bugle announced their arrival. He carefully moved along the long line of tables, checking each one for Georgio and his friend. Once or twice he thought he spotted them, but it turned out to be someone else. It was obvious to him that he was becoming a little over-anxious. He went into the *Jim Dandy* bar and had a quick drink to relax. When he finished, he resumed looking for them on the lower clubhouse landing.

He could still feel the wetness under his beard. It was beginning to irritate his neck. The suit was actually too heavy for this outing also.

Moving to the elevator, he went up to the second floor. It was even more crowded, and he arrived just as the first race was about to be called. He was caught up in a swarm of humanity and carried forward to the clubhouse railing. Flint found himself unwillingly sandwiched in next to a large woman in a red dress, who yelled wildly as the horses left the starting gate. She pounded her hand on the back of a smaller man standing at her side, who peered over the railing grim-faced while holding two tickets in his left hand.

She had an ear-bursting voice and Flint cupped his hands to his head to soften her screaming. It lasted until the horses had crossed the finish line. And with a series of oohs and ahs she moved away.

"We didn't make it, Miles...we didn't win."

"Thank God," the man replied. "I'd be dead if we had."

Flint laughed and moved on. The second floor contained a dining room; however, the outer portion was made up of box seats, mostly occupied by horse owners. He edged slowly along the rail. He didn't expect to find Georgio sitting in a clubhouse box, but he instinctively checked them out anyway.

It was well past the third race and he hadn't spotted them. He'd worked his way around the entire clubhouse with the exception of the top landing. This was exclusively for diners and he knew it would not be easy to walk around unnoticed. He first would have to gain entry to the area.

He walked up the flight of stairs to the top landing. Several couples were gathered near the head captain's counter waiting to be seated. He went up to the captain. "I have some friends sitting inside," he said with a straight face. "May I say hello to them? I won't be long."

"I'm sorry, sir," the captain answered. "We're very crowded this afternoon. I'll have one of the waitresses contact them for you. What table are they seated at?"

"They didn't say," Flint said directly. "I'll have to find them."

The captain gestured to the dining area. "As I said, we're really too full to let anyone roam around."

Flint extracted a fifty dollar bill from his pocket and held it so that the captain could plainly see it.

"I won't be but a minute," he insisted.

The captain nodded, took the money and waved Flint on. He looked the length of the dining area. Every table was filled, as he had found on the first floor, and waitresses were rushing everywhere. He didn't like this setup because he was too exposed. He had to walk between rows of tables instead of behind them, and the waitresses forced him to step aside each time they came by with a tray of food.

He was halfway down the main landing when he saw them. Georgio, Smith and their lady friend were seated at a table to the left. He stared and stared to make sure it was them. He was certain they would not recognize him, so he proceeded further, trying to get within earshot of their table. When he was but twenty feet away, Georgio turned and stared in his direction. Flint hesitated a second, but it was obvious that Georgio didn't notice him. The disguise was working, though under it Flint was sweltering.

He deliberately moved closer, hoping to pick up some of their conversation. As he passed their table slowly, he heard Smith say something to Georgio about placing their bets for the ninth race, and Georgio replied that it was still too early. Flint moved away, waited a minute or two and then came back in their direction. This time passing even closer to their table, he walked with a shuffle. The brunette was pointing with a forefinger as the horses for the third race entered the track.

Flint turned his head to catch what Georgio was saying and suddenly, as if hit by a football player, a waitress opened a kitchen door to his left, swinging out with a large tray in her right hand, and crashed into Flint. The force knocked him completely over onto Georgio's table. The table collapsed under his weight and all four landed on the wooden floor. Flint's sweaty beard popped off during his fall, and when he sat up he was staring Georgio directly in the face. The mustached cop turned white, as if seeing a ghost. Flint quickly reached for Georgio, but the cop jumped back, turned, and began running for the stairwell. Flint was on his feet in a moment, and forgetting Smith and the girl, took off after Georgio.

The bewildered diners and waitresses scrambled about, but the immediate impact of the incident was over before security guards could react.

Flint saw Georgio run down to the lower level. He pursued him into a crowd at the betting windows in the clubhouse. He had to push and shove his way between the bettors, as did Georgio in his haste to escape from Flint.

Flint almost caught up to him at the turnstile, but Georgio vaulted over a white fence and ran for the paddock area. Flint followed him over the fence. At this point two Pinkerton guards began chasing Georgio and Flint.

Flint kept watching as Georgio's head popped up here and there in the crowd near the paddock. Georgio then crossed to the tree-lined lawn and headed for the exit gate on Union Avenue. Flint cut through the jockey building walkway in an attempt to head him off. He rounded the end of the building and spotted Georgio coming at an angle across the lawn.

"Stop...stop, Georgio," he shouted.

Georgio paused, looked in his direction and drew a gun and began firing. The spectators screamed and ran for cover, and Flint ducked behind the corner of the jockey house as two or three bullets ripped into its siding.

When he looked again, Georgio was running once more toward the exit. Flint sprang forward and then crashed to the ground. A plainclothes security officer had tripped him. Flint jumped up and the officer grabbed him around the shoulders. Flint spun him off, but the officer grabbed him again. Then another officer came up and grabbed Flint. He could see Georgio moving quickly out through the exit.

"Let go! Let go!" Flint yelled. "He's getting away...the man you want is out there."

"Yeah, Buddy," the larger of the two men remarked. "You just relax, and we'll see what this is all about."

"You're making a mistake," Flint insisted.

"Let's go to the security office and discuss it," was the reply.

Flint couldn't move. They had his arms pinned tight, and then one of them clamped handcuffs on his wrists. The next time Flint looked, Georgio was no longer in sight.

The head of NYRA Security was a tall, thin man in his mid-forties, dressed in a well-tailored pale blue suit. He looked more like a horse owner than a security officer. Flint eyed him cautiously as the room they had taken him to at the back of the main grandstand filled up with security personnel.

No one said anything at first. They all seemed to be waiting for something.... Eventually the door opened and another uniformed Pinkerton guard entered, carrying a brown paper bag.

The well-dressed officer reached in the bag and took out Flint's fake beard and threw it on a table. "Explain this," he said in a soft, firm voice.

Flint smiled back. "I was going to play a joke on someone. It backfired."

"What sort of joke?"

"An old friend I hadn't seen in some time. We used to play tricks on each other in college."

The officer wiggled his nose and looked closer at Flint. "What's you friend's name?"

"Tom Smith," Flint snapped back.

"Where's he from?"

"What's it matter?" asked Flint.

"It matters a lot," said the officer. "Your friend

had a gun. He shot into the crowd near the pad-dock. It matters a lot to me to know who he is."

Flint sat up straighter. "Oh, that guy! That wasn't my friend. I don't know who that guy was."

"Is that why you were chasing him?"

"Was I chasing him?" Flint inquired in a muffled voice.

"You can say anything you like," the officer said. "I'm in no hurry. My people are in no hurry. And I'm certain if we don't get any straight answers here, we will get some when we go downtown to the local authorities. It's up to you to cooperate."

"It sounds like an ultimatum," Flint said.

"No. It isn't," the officer continued. "We'd just like some honest answers. We'd also like to identify the man and woman your friend was seated with in the dining area."

"I have no idea who they were," Flint blurted back.

"I can see we're getting nowhere," the officer said. "Well, let's begin with you. What's your real name and why were you in the clubhouse alone?"

Flint grunted. "Look, inspector, or whatever your title is. I want to see my lawyer before I answer any more questions. Do you mind?"

"You haven't answered any questions as far as I'm concerned."

"Look," warned Flint, "you've got nothing to detain me on. Some guy runs out of your club-house, shoots at anyone within sight, and leaves the track. He was the one with the gun. I didn't do anything but run around. Have you got a law against running within the track? I don't believe so!"

"You wrecked the table," the man insisted.

"Fine," admitted Flint. "I have a sore neck and bad shoulder from the bump the waitress gave me when she came flying out of the kitchen without looking where she was going. I'll get my doctor to look at it, and I'll get my lawyer to sue for damages. Now who's right and who's wrong here?"

The security officer stood up and looked at his co-workers. "You've made your point, Mister. Maybe I can't hold you, but I can ask you to leave the track. We have that much authority. I'm sure you know where the gate is?"

Flint lifted himself from the chair and slowly walked to the door. He continued to walk slowly until he was out on Union Avenue. Then he made a dash for a pay phone and called Blake. He explained his altercation at the track. Blake said he still hadn't received any reports from Benson. Flint told him to warn Benson that he felt certain Georgio would be trying to cover his tracks, and that Marty's place would no doubt be Georgio's next stop. He told Blake that he also was heading for Marty's.

"I'll bring help," Blake offered.

"Not just yet," Flint said. "Too much activity might scare Georgio off. I'll call when it's time."

"Be careful," warned Blake. "And if you can't reach me by phone, call Siro's and give a message to Davis. He can be trusted. Davis will reach me."

"I'm not sure I want anyone else privy to this," Flint insisted.

Blake reassured him. "You can tell Davis anything. Besides, it's safer than these direct calls, don't you agree?"

"If you say so, Doc," Flint said."

"One more thing," Blake added. "That piece of trash in Sandy's basement was removed to the New York City morgue. Would you believe no one has claimed it yet?"

"I hope he enjoys a long undiscovered sleep," Flint mused. "Take care, Doc. We'll be in touch."

Flint called Saratoga Taxi and waited impatiently for the cab to arrive. His anger was growing. He also felt humiliation inside for having bungled things at the track. It was an amateurish performance at best. Then his thoughts turned again to Georgio.

The jigsaw events of the past few weeks were suddenly falling into place.

It was all very logical now in retrospect, Flint was thinking. Why had it taken so long to figure out? Perhaps the simple solutions are simply just that, too plainly clear to be recognized and uncovered. But still thinking about it, Flint cursed himself for not following one of his basic rules. Suspect everyone and anyone. Even your best friends, until proven innocent.

Georgio's hidden ambition should have been recognized. Silently, while waiting for the taxi, Flint was struck with the realization that perhaps Monica's observations were proving correct. "He was getting too old for this game."

The taxi appeared at the curb and Flint, jumping quickly into the back seat, ordered the driver to proceed to Marty's place.

He wasn't sure of the outcome, but he was pretty certain it was near showdown time for him and Georgio.

As the Taxi left the paved road and rumbled down the long dirt road toward Marty's house, Flint reached under his pant leg and removed a small revolver from its holster. The NYRA security people hadn't even bothered to search him, which, considering Georgio's actions, surprised him. It was baffling to him how they operated, especially letting him go so easily. He didn't think his argument was all that convincing or strong.

He departed the taxi three hundred yards from the house. It was still daylight, but the heavily treed land around Marty's all but shut out the sun, and one would have thought it was much later.

Flint half walked and half crawled in the direction right of the house where Benson was supposed to be. He couldn't see any cars or hear any noises. It was like walking through a jungle. He reached a position that looked like the right spot but Benson wasn't there. He moved further to the right, climbing a small slope which had a thick clump of trees. The silence of the moment was broken by a car motor. Flint grabbed a tree branch and raised himself, just in time to see the long, sleek Cadillac pull into Marty's drive. Someone ran from the driver's seat into the house, kicking the front door as he ran. He heard a scream and a gunshot.

Flint's nerves jumped. "God," he muttered, "he's killed my witness."

Flint came on a dead run to the house. Without the least bit of concern for his own safety, he flew through the door into the living room, his revolver held forward in search of Georgio.

"Hello, big boy," the familiar voice called out. Flint spun around. Marty, propped up in a chair, squinted back at him with the same red, swollen eyes he remembered from their first meeting.

"How's tricks, big boy?"

He couldn't believe it, but he found himself saying, "Where's Georgio?"

A figure appeared in the back doorway. Flint trained his gun in that direction and dropped on one knee to the floor.

"I got him, Mr. Flint. I got him," Benson's voice traveled across the room. Under his right arm he clung to Georgio's neck. Georgio's finely groomed, mustached face looked like a balloon ready to burst as Benson increased his grip.

"Easy on him," Flint warned. "We need him alive."

"I will...w-w-will, Mr. Flint," Benson stammered. "The b-bbum won't get way from m-m-me."

Flint turned to Marty. "Well, what do you think of your Main Man now?"

Her face wrinkled up in a furious glare. "The S.O.B. tried to kill me...he really tried to kill me!"

Flint gazed around the smelly room and then back at Marty. She was rotting away from drugs, but with the proper care she might even make it through all this, he thought. If she did, it would take a miracle.

There was no need to call Blake's contact, Davis. Flint picked up Marty's phone and called Blake direct.

"It's all over Doc," he said joyfully. "And I had nothing to do with it. Benson did it all. Give me time to clear out of here, then call the local cops. Marty isn't interested in holding anymore parties, I reckon. I'll secure Georgio and leave Benson with him until they get here. Thanks so much for all your help. I'll get in touch later and I'll have Sandy call you. Hope we can get together under more pleasant circumstances."

"Will you be leaving Saratoga immediately?" asked Blake.

"Right after the ninth race," said Flint. "I've got a hunch triple I want to play. Something tells me I'm going to get rich today. By the way, have the locals call this special New York City number -- 544-6000 -- tell them to talk to Harry Waite. He'll fill them in on Georgio. Be good, Doc."

21. The Ninth Race

The late afternoon sun sprayed its long rays across the maples and pines at the Saratoga track, leaving streaks of lavender on the white grandstands. Large swans fluttered freely about its center pond, and wave upon wave of people roamed up and down near the rail as the ninth race approached.

Flint, staying clear of the clubhouse, went into the far end of the grandstand and leaning against a post, took the film strip from his pocket and held it up to a nearby light.

There were twelve possible combinations of three numbers each. He read them forward, then backward. He couldn't figure which one to play. He studied it further. He took a pencil and paper and tried to rearrange the numbers. He took the first numbers and then the second numbers and tried to put them into sequence, but nothing made any sense.

He went to the bar and ordered a drink and looked more closely at the numbers. The bell rang and he looked at the monitor, with but three minutes to race time. Turning back, his arm hit his glass, spilling the drink over the piece of paper. The numbers disappeared before his eyes as the paper soaked up the drink. Then, while he was still watching, three new numbers appeared on the paper...*11-4-7*. He examined the paper. It was apparently made of special fabric that he hadn't noticed before. He ran to the pari-mutuel window and planked down a fifty dollar bill. "Give me twenty-five triples on *11-4-7*," he ordered.

He watched the race from the upper stretch, mingling with the one-dollar family bettors, whose kids scrambled back and forth in a wild flurry of chase-the-other-kid.

He couldn't see too clearly and he couldn't hear the P.A. system. He stepped up on a bench and was able to see the last thundering drive around the turn and into the stretch, but he couldn't make out the post numbers. The crowd leaped and chanted and yelled. Finally they settled down to wait for the results. There was a photo finish for first place, which delayed the results. Then, in an earthquake-like rumble he heard the shouting and cheering as the results were flashed on the infield board...*11-4-7* in that order.

"How much did it pay?" someone shouted to a steward. "How much was the triple?"

"Six thousand and change," the steward yelled back. "A big one."

Flint felt the wad of triple tickets in his pocket. Roughly one hundred fifty thousand dollars worth. Beads of moisture stood out on his forehead, and the thought of all that money made him vaguely uncomfortable. There was no way he could cash them in, so in a slow stride he drifted out of the track with the huge crowd onto Union Avenue.

Across from the track he went to a pay booth near *Scotty's Paddock Bar* and without hesitation, called Monica's place in California. The maid answered the phone.

"No, Mr. Flint," she apologized. "Miss Monica is at the studio working on a new TV series. Miss

216

Sandy is here, though."

"Let me talk to her," Flint said.

While he waited for Sandy to come to the phone, he watched the long line of spectators leaving the track. Cars moved slowly up and down Union Avenue as if their bumpers were welded to one another. "How are you?" he finally heard Sandy's soft, excited voice on the line. "I've missed you terribly, Flint."

"It's so good to hear your voice," he told her.

"Is everything all right?" she asked.

"Everything is fine, my sweet, just fine."

"When are you coming back?" she asked.

"Well," he answered, "that all depends on you."

"There was a short pause. "I...I don't understand," she said.

"I was thinking that perhaps you'd like to come back to Saratoga...at least for the balance of the racing season? Would you?"

"Is it possible now?" she inquired.

"It's very possible, my dear."

Then she said, "You found Robin's killer, didn't you?"

"Yes. My work here is over. We got our man."

"I prayed you would."

"Tell you what," he said, "I'll give you all the assorted details over the most expensive meal I can buy in Saratoga. I'll call you later when Monica gets home, and we'll make flight arrangements... The weather here is super and I have a few extra bucks to spend as long as I can find someone to to cash in my tickets."

"What tickets?"

"Oh," he replied, "a little bonus I received for this assignment. I've got to find some retired citizens to do my cashing in, though."

"I don't understand," said Sandy.

"It's too complicated to explain now. It has something to do with the tax bite. Trust me."

"Take care, my love," she said. "I'll be waiting for your call. Monica is expected about 8:30, our time."

"I love you," he said once more. "I love you very much."

"I love you too."

Shadows were lengthening across the green background of the track as he stepped out of the phone booth. Still, the air was warm and humid. People passing by all seemed to be smiling, except for one solemn-faced man standing outside *Scotty's* who was an apparent loser for the day.

Then Flint realized that life was exactly that --one big gamble. Saratoga, with its unique magnetism, its emotion, its beauty, exemplified it all.

Happy and relaxed, he walked to downtown Saratoga.

-- The End --